Cliff Hanger

A Running Scared Suspense

Laurie A. Perkins

Cliff Hanger
A Running Scared Suspense

ISBN 978-0-557-01719-5

Acknowledgements

I would like to thank the many people who helped make my second book possible.

My exceptional husband Phil, my first editor and encourager.

My writer's group friend, Clare Schoenfeld, who read my story over two years giving me wonderful feedback and encouragement.

My friend Vivian Cate, who read my book and critiqued it with great insight.

My sister Beverly Danielka, niece Marlo Roberts, friend Beth Harrington, and John Alger for their suggestions that helped improve my book.

A special thanks to my family who read the earliest version of Cliff Hanger under a different title, and liked it enough to encourage me to continue to publication.

Dedication

To Clare Schoenfeld and Vivian Cate,
writer friends who gave their time to help me accomplish
my dream.

Chapter 1

Jessie cautiously glanced around as she exited the bus in front of the old two-story brick terminal. *So this is Red Fish, Oklahoma,* she noted with a sigh. She had been traveling for two days. Another half day and she would be safe. Sweat beaded her forehead. She removed her hat and jacket, tucking them through the handles of her duffel, and walked quickly inside. Immediately the temperature dropped. The hot Oklahoma sun couldn't penetrate the impressive building that housed second floor business offices and the amenities of the bus station. She checked the posted schedule for Tucson. *A three-hour wait?* Jessie frowned. *Too long!* She slipped out the front door and studied her surroundings. The one main street of the small western town was lined with two and three story buildings of many shapes and shades of color. A scattering of pickup trucks and cars were parked at the curbs in front of a variety of stores. Few people were out in the heat. Everything looked normal. *Now what should I do?* Her stomach growled reminding her it was nearly lunchtime. She'd eaten her last granola bar and was tired of vending machine food. At least eating would help her fill the time waiting for the next bus.

"Excuse me." The ticket agent looked up. "Is there someplace nearby where I could get lunch?"

"Out the door, turn right and down one block. Go there all the time myself. It's called The Three Sisters Cafe."

"Thanks." Her duffle bag dragged on her arm. *No sense carrying this around.*

Jessie found a wall of lockers just inside the front door of the station. She stuffed her Visa card and emergency cash into her jeans pocket then thrust her fanny pack, coat and hat in the duffle bag and crammed it into one of the lockers. Everything was now safely stashed. Unencumbered, she went out the door, turned, and soon found the cafe. Jessie slid into a booth near the back where she could still see out its large windows. Studying the menu, she ordered a cheeseburger special. As she glanced up from the now empty plate, a black car crept down the street toward the bus station. Fear tore through her. *I have to get out of here. I can't wait for the bus.*

Jessie looked at the bill the waitress was handing her, laid all her cash out and asked, "Is there a car rental around here?"

"Down two blocks on the right at the edge of town."

"Thanks. Do you have a back door?"

"Are you ok?"

"Old boyfriend I'm trying to avoid," Jessie improvised.

"Through the kitchen. Let me show you."

Jessie darted out the door down an alley and cautiously worked her way out to the main road. There it was, only a few buildings away." *I can do this…I'm in control.*

Before she arrived at the car rental, the sidewalk stopped, forcing her to walk on the berm. Jessie could hear cars drive up behind her, passing within inches. *Just as long as it isn't that black car,* she thought with a shiver. She didn't even turn to look. She stepped off the roadway and onto the grassy edge. She hated the feeling of vulnerability out in the open like this. Jessie picked up her pace, eyes straight ahead, focused on her destination. If only she could take pleasure in being in this wide-open country. She usually loved to travel. It lifted her spirits, but not today. She had to keep moving. Wind blew gritty dirt into her face. She rubbed her eyes.

Suddenly, her way was blocked. A man grabbed her arms and pulled her to the side, away from the road.

Oh, no! They found me! She looked up and gasped in surprise, "What…? Who are you?"

Stunned, she wondered, *is he saving me from being hit?* The man pinned her against the hood of a car. *He isn't saving me*, she thought, *he's attacking me.*

"Stop it! You're hurting me!" she cried. When the man's grip loosened on her wrists, she rolled out from under him. Jessie didn't look back but dashed for cover in the sparse trees that edged the road. She'd barely reached the first trees when he caught her around the waist. She found herself hanging in mid-air, feet dangling.

"Put me down!" she yelled, struggling against him. He held her back against his chest as he walked toward the car; her flailing fists couldn't hit him. *What can I do*? Panic filled her. *My feet! I can use my feet.* She swung her right foot back, hitting him hard on the shin.

Swearing, he thrust her down, turned her around and grabbed her wrists with one hand. This time, he held her away from his legs. She looked up into eyes filled with anger.

"What do you think you're doing?" she gasped. "Help!" she screamed, "Help! I'm being kidnapped!" The highway was deserted. The car rental office wasn't far. *Maybe they'll hear me*, she thought. "Fire! Kidnap! Help!"

A rough hand abruptly covered her mouth and nose, clamping down so hard she couldn't breathe. Panic again surged through her. Claustrophobia threatened to overwhelm her. *Is he going to smother me?* Pulling one of her hands free, she tore at his hand over her face, all the while screaming inside, *why is he doing this to me? He's not one of those following me…is he?*

"Look, lady," he said as he struggled to hold her writhing body, "I'm not gonna hurt you. Shut up and stop kicking or I'll have to do something more drastic!"

He took his hand away from her mouth and grabbed her free arm as she gasped for air.

"I've been hunting you for days, and I'm not going to let you get away now."

Jessie took gulping deep breaths.

Reaching into his pocket, he warned, "I wouldn't try screaming again, unless you want to be chewing on this." He held up a sweat soaked soiled rag, passing it under her nose. Jessie gagged.

Still holding her wrists in one large hand, he tucked the rag back in his pocket and reached into the pockets of her faded denim jeans, pulling out their contents.

He laid the items on the car hood: a locker key, her Visa card, and a handful of tissues. He stuffed the tissues back in her jeans, but kept the rest.

"Can't have you carrying around anything that can pick a lock," he said with a frown.

Locks? What does he mean locks? And why would this thug be hunting me?

He reached into his other pocket and pulled out a set of handcuffs, quickly snapping them onto her wrists. She was trapped securely before she realized it. Sharp fear, like needles of electricity, burst from the pit of her stomach and shot through her body. She sagged.

Lifting and pulling her around the car, he dragged her toward the open door and pushed her into the front seat. Jessie shook her head to clear the fog of shock. *I've got to fight back. I can't let this happen.*

The thug reached across her with the seatbelt, fumbling for the slot to clip it in. As his arm inched closer and closer she lunged forward and bit into his bicep – hard.

"You bite like a spaniel!" he spat. He jerked his arm away from her aching jaws, her bite barely fazing him. His muscles were like rock. He finished latching her in, successfully trapping her hands in her lap. Perspiration ran down her body, intensifying the sweet musk of her perfume. A spicy odor lingered where he'd brushed against her. Closing the door, he slid into his seat and started the car.

"You Neanderthal!" she sputtered. "What do you mean you've been hunting me? What kind of person are you?"

"A broke one," he retorted. He put the car in gear and started forward.

"Hunting people? It's barbaric!"

Stomping on the brakes, he whipped around to face her. "Listen, I don't always like some of my assignments. Especially chasing down rich runaways for their overbearing mothers."

"Runaway! I'm not running away." *Not from my mom at any rate. What could he mean?* "My mom isn't even alive any more. She died four years ago."

"Sorry lady, but I'm not listening to your lies." He turned back, stepping on the gas. "Your mother said you'd have some wild stories. Don't get any ideas of sweet-talking your way out of this. When I'm on a case, nothing gets in my way."

"Who the heck are you anyway? Are you with the police?" She was frantic. She couldn't trust the police.

"I'm K.C. Avalon," he said with pride, thrusting out a decidedly square chin. "Owner of Avalon Investigative Services. You, Miss Jessica Jean Overton, are my ticket to getting my life back on track. Hunting hasn't been good lately."

"Where are you taking me?"

"Back home to your mother, of course." They pulled onto the main highway and headed north.

If only I could go home to my mom. Jessie was near tears. *Jen and I could always count on her help when we had problems…and this problem topped them all. Well, almost.*

"As I told you before, my mother is no longer living."

Her mom and dad's retirement dream was to move from the frigid winters of North Dakota to Tucson. Then suddenly, her mom became sick, and just as unexpectedly, she was gone.

"I spoke to her personally," he said.

"You couldn't have. I told you she's dead."

"Well, she hired me to find her daughter."

"Tell me, just who is supposed to be my 'mother'?"

"Don't you know your own mother?" K.C. exclaimed with disgust. "You rich kids today, your moms and dads marry and divorce over and over so even you can't keep track. Your mother, Mrs. Olivia Spaulding, contacted me personally and asked me to find her runaway daughter."

"My last name isn't even Spaulding!"

"She told me you were suffering from depression since your divorce and the two of you had an argument over your inheritance."

"Depression? Divorce?"

"After you ran away, she found her diamond pendant missing."

"That's ridiculous!"

"She wants her necklace back. She's willing to forgive all when I bring you home."

"No! Don't take me there."

Her kidnapper ignored her and continued driving.

Jessie shuddered, closing her eyes. Mrs. Spaulding must have discovered she'd been hiding in the summerhouse behind her mansion.

One of the things Jessie learned from her mom was to go the "extra mile." She had been expected to set the example for her kid sister. Jennifer was three years younger than she, a mere youngster at twenty-five. Now, Jen had everything Jessie had ever wanted: a wonderful husband, a new baby, and living in balmy California. It just wasn't fair. *I should never have run to New England to finish my education.* Jessie pushed down feelings of loss and betrayal as she remembered how she had gotten herself into this predicament. Memories of that day intruded as she sank into despair.

***

"Michael Spaulding. I want to see you before you leave class!" Jessie commanded in her firmest teacher's voice. He gave the cliché "spaced out" new meaning. He was in another world most of the time. She almost wished he'd do something that would get him into trouble, just so she'd know if he felt anything.

Michael slowly reached for his backpack and made his way toward her desk, shirt hanging out of his oversized cargo pants. He looked like a poor lost waif, even though he came from one of the wealthiest families in town. His black hair tumbled into his eyes. He rarely smiled. Michael could be a good student, but he just didn't seem to care. Her concern for him led her to be somewhat lenient, but that didn't mean he could get away with skipping his homework assignments.

"Ya, Miss Overton?" Michael stood in front of her desk, his hands stuffed into his pockets, his backpack slung low on his back. He was bodily present but uninterested.

"Michael, you haven't completed your history homework. This is the fourth time this month. What is wrong?"

"Nothin'," Michael replied.

"Do you need special help? You could ask your mother to help you?" she persisted.

"Naw, I can't ask her, she's busy." He shifted from one foot to the other, gazing past her head at something outside the window.

She also looked out the window. All Jessie saw were puffy white clouds scudding across the sky and new spring grass struggling to grow in hardened crisscrossed paths.

"Michael, look at me." Jessie drew his attention back to her. "You need to get this work done. If you don't, you could fail tenth grade."

Michael's family was wealthy in material things, but he lacked the love and guidance of a father. Apparently Mr. Spaulding had disappeared several years ago, before Jessie had come to Inglweiss Academy to teach. Michael's mother took over the family business. Now, it seemed, that very business kept Mrs. Spaulding from being available to Michael when he needed her most.

"Michael, is your mother home today? I'd like to come by and talk with her."

"Ya, she has some business to deal with at the house. Ma said I should go to the mall after school." He was now gazing out the open classroom door watching the students coming and going to their classes.

"Well, I think I'll stop by after school and see if we can have a chat about your homework problem."

Michael looked as if he could care less what she did. He shifted again from one leg to the other.

"Oh, go ahead and go, Michael," she said, shaking her head in frustration. Michael's mother never came to the parent/teacher meetings. If Mrs. Spaulding wouldn't come to the school, Jessie would just have to go there. It couldn't be too much out of her way. Jessie watched him shuffle out the door as the next class began to file in.

***

"...not much out of my way," Jessie mumbled. That had been a huge understatement. Her reasons for visiting Mrs. Spaulding at the time were honorable...weren't they?

Jessie prided herself on caring for her students, and she had really been concerned about Michael's schoolwork. That was only one of the reasons. She knew how important it was to have caring parents, and Michael needed a loving parent to care about him. She'd hoped to encourage Mrs. Spaulding to be there for him.

I was only thinking of helping him she told herself. *Pride*, her mind argued, *you thought you knew better and foolishly rushed in. Now look where it got you.*

What seemed like a slight detour on behalf of a needy student had turned into a nightmare.

Chapter 2

When Jessie had visited parents in previous schools they had lived in modest homes or apartments. She enjoyed driving through the quaint neighborhoods where children played in friends' yards and parents visited each other. Driving to Michael's house revealed something quite different. Quaint neighborhoods disappeared and expanses of lawn with mammoth houses filled the countryside. Jessie instantly slowed down and gawked – she couldn't help herself. Everett's elite Inglweiss Academy catered to wealthy families but she hadn't realized just how wealthy. Winding driveways, acres of beautifully landscaped lawns, sprawling homes made of brick and stone with turrets and porches mesmerized her. White balustrades were everywhere. *I bet no one knows his or her neighbors.* The homes were more like castles and the Spaulding Mansion was largest of all. Many of the homes had fences, but the gate and walls around Michael's home rivaled the Great Wall of China. Jessie parked her blue Toyota at the entrance of the vine-covered walls.

She stepped out of the car, locked it and slipped her keys into her skirt pocket. The high stone wall rose before her. Thrusting skyward from the top of the walls were tall black metal prongs that ended in spear shaped tips. The wall and its imposing hardware surrounded the entire mansion. The massiveness of the estate was overpowering. She had no doubt the threatening ramparts discouraged intruders.

Jessie peered through the gates at a wide expanse of lawn. Quince and forsythia were starting to bloom. Oak, maple and pine trees were placed purposefully around the lawn. She tried to see beyond them, then realized the landscaping had been designed to hide the mansion. Still, parts of the house towered above the huge oaks and maples.

Where she could see through the trees, she recognized rhododendrons and azaleas along the surrounding walls. A large wooded area stretched to the left of the house. She thought she saw something white near the woods, a building of some sort. The main house itself was magnificent. Daffodils, yellow heads nodding in a breeze, grew at the feet of yew shrubs in front of the house. The springtime colors and foliage alleviated the harsh look of its weathered gray stone facade.

Near the gate, Jessie spied a small black box attached to the stone pillar, a security intercom system. *I hope Mrs. Spaulding is home... for Michael's sake*, she told herself. She realized later that pride in being the perfect, caring teacher was her downfall.

The driveway circled in front of the mansion where several cars were parked. Jessie leaned against the gates for a better look, stumbling when they noisily swung open. *Did they hear me?* She looked around, no doors opened and there wasn't anyone around the grounds. *Looks like an invitation to enter.*

Straightening the jacket of her peach wool suit, she pushed the strap of her small beige leather purse higher onto her shoulder, slipped through the gate, and walked confidently up the drive toward the front door. The bright sunshine was unusual for early May in upstate New York. It gave her confidence as well as pleasure.

Other parts of the house sprawled across the landscaped tableau as she drew nearer. All was quiet as she stood at the door and gazed up, up, up at the massive manor. Abruptly, her confidence disappeared. The house was awe-inspiring. Its multi-paned windows, like huge dark eyes, made her feel like someone was watching her. In the center of the large double doors, there was an intricately designed coat of arms of brass heraldry with horses' heads and horseshoes against a checkered shield. Jessie looked for a bell or knocker to announce her presence. Unexpectedly she heard a woman's firm voice, then a man's, pleading. She turned toward the sound.

"I…tell you…" the man shuddered. I…I didn't take it!"

The woman's voice purred seductively, "Now, Edward, you know I won't accept stealing in my organization. Lying about it only compounds the sin."

"But, I…I didn't steal it!" Edward implored, "I told you, when Miggs came by, he told me there wasn't a drop this time. I…I couldn't believe it. There's always something. But…but Miggs insisted there wasn't." The quiver of fear in Edward's voice was growing more noticeable.

"Edward, if you don't have the money," the woman's voice hardened, "who does?"

Jessie had moved toward the voices then realized she was eavesdropping. *I think I'll come back later.* She didn't like what she'd heard about stealing. *What about Michael?* Jessie's thoughts warred with each other. *He needs help. What should I do?* She wanted to let the people inside know she was there, but a doorbell wasn't obvious. Turning back to the entrance, she studied it once more. One of the horseshoes looked like a doorknocker. She was reaching for it, when the voices rose alarmingly. Jessie jumped at the sharp crack of a slap that sounded as if it were right next to her.

"Olivia…please, it…wasn't me," the man's voice sobbed. "Ask Miggs. He's the only one I know who might…have an idea."

Her hand stopped at the name, Olivia. The woman with the silky voice that dripped with venom was Michael's mother.

Unconsciously, she pressed herself against the door, listening as the voices continued.

"Edward, we did ask Miggs and he says it was your idea. Of course, Miggs can't be here to verify your story. Seems he's had a very nasty accident." Olivia's voice continued its smooth delivery even as her words threatened. "Take him out back," she commanded someone in the room. "You know what to do!"

"No...please...I...didn't..." The man's begging voice trailed away with the shuffle of feet.

Without thinking, Jessie slipped to the left side of the house as she heard movement inside. Beyond the shrubbery, the first of the many-paned windows was open. No wonder she'd heard the altercation so well. Hunching over behind the bushes, she peeked inside. Standing in the center of a very large and ornately paneled library, Jessie saw the back of a woman. She was immaculately dressed in a tailored black suit. Her black curls, so like Michael's, were neatly coifed. That had to be Olivia. She was tall and slim, with a body that belies a woman in her mid forties. When the woman turned toward the patio doors at the rear of the room, Jessie saw her more clearly. What would have been a beautiful face was twisted with hate. But it was the terrifying ferocity of Olivia Spaulding's eyes that really shook Jessie.

Jessie heard a low chuckle as Mrs. Spaulding turned to someone nearby. A uniformed Everett policeman lounged on an overstuffed sofa watching with a smirk as two men in dark suits pushed another man toward the patio doors. If Jessie didn't move, they would soon be outside and might see her lurking in the shrubbery. She looked back to the front door, and then to the grove of trees off to her left where she had seen a white structure earlier. Now she could see it was a green and white hexagonal summerhouse tucked into the grove of spruce and maple trees. A scream from inside the mansion frightened her into action. Jessie ran for the door of the building, fumbling with the handle. *What if it's locked?* The latch opened, and Jessie slipped inside just as the men came through the patio doors, dragging the frantic man between them. They headed toward the woods behind her hiding place. Jessie held her breath as she watched through the slatted blinds of the summerhouse. Her heart was pounding. She stood very still. *Lord, don't let them find me.*

"Please, I didn't do it!" Edward begged. "Please! Please!"

Jessie caught a glimpse of the men holding Edward. Their expressions were cold, unmoving and one had a terrible scar on his face. Only their eyes revealed emotion. They glowed with the fire of excitement and anticipation. Jessie sensed an unrelenting darkness surrounding Edward's captors – their hair, their eyes, their suits, and their faces reflected a terrible, terrible darkness. She understood in a chilling way what the word ruthless meant.

Edging her way to the back of the summerhouse she continued to watch through the blinds. Edward had stopped struggling. She was mesmerized as she watched them drag the weeping man to the edge of the woods. Suddenly, she heard a noise behind her. Turning with a jerk, she moved silently along the side of the building toward the door. As she lifted the edge of one of the blinds, Jessie saw Mrs. Spaulding and the policeman turn from the patio and enter the door to the library. *They watched and did nothing.* Jessie couldn't believe it. Just as patio door closed, a shot rang out. Jessie gasped. A chill of fear left her weak as it coursed up and down her spine. In spite of her wool suit, she stood shivering.

Once again Jessie crept to where she had seen the men drag Edward. He was lying on the ground, a growing blossom of blood spreading across his chest. The two men dragged Edward off into the trees, leaving a scarlet trail.

Jessie felt nauseated. Tendrils of hair stuck to her face, and, as she pushed them away, she realized tears were pouring down her cheeks. Jessie collapsed onto the round bench in the center of the summerhouse and buried her face in her hands. Her purse strap slipped from her shoulder, and fell to the floor. As she sat in numbed shock the voices of the returning men shook her into action. Again, Jessie silently made her way to the shutters and watched.

"Well, that's done," snickered the shorter of the two as he smoothed his rumpled jacket. They reentered the house.

Jessie waited for nearly twenty minutes, until she heard car doors slam. Two of the three cars in the driveway sped around the circle and out the gate.

Cautiously, she opened the summerhouse door. The trees and bushes offered hiding places and protection. She slipped off her high-heeled shoes and ran. From tree to bush, around the right wall of the estate, away from the woods, away from the summerhouse, away from the now closed patio doors. She headed for the gate and safety. Numb with shock and fear, she was only faintly aware of the cold sharp stones and grass beneath her feet. Jessie finally came to the rhododendron next to the gate. How would she get out? The gate was now firmly shut. She looked from the house to the gate then noticed a release latch that would open the gate from the inside. She crept to the gate and grasped the latch, lifting it. The gate creaked loudly, prompting her to move faster. Jessie quickly latched the gate and glanced towards the library window in time to see a face turn away. Whirling around, she ran to her car.

Chapter 3

K.C. took a quick look at his captive. At last she was quiet. His grip loosened on the steering wheel. The Overton girl appeared smaller now since her arms and legs weren't flailing about. She was looking straight ahead. Occasionally he'd glance at the young woman. Every time, her animated face held different expressions, some of them filled with fear. *What could she be thinking*, he wondered? *Do I really want to know?*

She must have sensed his glances. Her head turned; for a second she looked directly at him. Tears glistened at the edges of the deep brown eyes fixed on his. Slowly her gaze returned to the window ahead. She shivered. Though outwardly she was passive, in that fleeting look, he recognized terror.

What did she have to be frightened of? She was wealthy. She could have anything she wanted. Family problems weren't his concern. He just does the job he's hired to do. Now if he had her money, he'd have no more worries. Instead, here he was, the thirty-two year old owner of a struggling investigative business, filling in with retrieving runaways just to make ends meet.

The rustling of his captive suggested his passive passenger was stirring out of her daydream. Or was it a nightmare? She struggled to sit up straighter.

"How can anyone choose to hunt people?" she mumbled. It was almost as if she had read his mind.

At first he didn't bother to answer. What could he say? Every acceptable job by his parent's standards just didn't work out for one reason or another. No matter what the profession or what the hours, he always felt like he was barely existing in the tedium of life. Where would that take him? Not where he wanted to go. He wanted something more.

"Well?" she persisted.

"I just fell into it."

"Since when do you just fall into something that teaches you to kidnap someone? Was it a major offered in the college you attended?"

"Did you major in insults?" he countered. "I didn't choose college."

"So it was your parents?"

At least she's talking, he thought. "Yah. I couldn't stand being stuck in one place like a college campus. I nearly quit several times."

"Why didn't you?"

"If it hadn't been for the wrestling team in college I would have gone nuts."

"What about normal jobs?"

"Normal jobs? Eh!" he grunted in disgust. "When I worked as a manager at a bank, nine to five, day in and day out, I could have screamed. I just couldn't see myself spending the rest of my life doing that. Teaching school wasn't much better. Night after night of preparation throughout endless days, just trying to get young people to care enough to learn."

"I'm a teacher. It's been my passion since I was a little girl. That's why I'm in this mess."

"A rich girl like you, a teacher?"

She sighed. "I told you, I'm not rich."

"If I had your money, I wouldn't need this job."

"No nine to five for you then. That only left harassment and kidnapping. Well that's logical."

"You asked."

Her probing only reminded him of the frustration he had experienced with those jobs. They had been so confining. There was nothing but rules and other peoples' expectations. Satisfaction for him was zilch. It had been like that for a long, long time. Struggling, always struggling to find some peace. *At least I have my looks and strength.*

He'd worked hard developing the muscles he'd so admired in others. During high school he went to the Y three days a week, sometimes more. He loved working through the Nautilus machines one after another. When other members saw him coming, they stepped out of his way. One trainer said he attacked those machines with "single-minded fury." From Nautilus he moved on to conquer the barbells. His bodybuilding had been the one thing that had given him an edge over other guys. No one would dare take him on. I'm definitely no wimp! K.C. thought, smiling in satisfaction.

Glancing at her again, he saw her eyes had closed, long lashes curled onto her cheeks. K.C. tried not to waken her as he continued down Route 44. He took a deep breath, savoring the sweet scent that radiated from her. She wasn't bad looking, maybe a foot shorter than his 6'2". Her sandy blond hair brushed the edges of her chin just like one of those servant boys in the stories of castles and knights. No servant boy ever had a figure like that. The red t-shirt fit nicely in all the right places. Her blue jeans weren't new but were obviously comfortable. What seemed out of place were her manacled hands lying in her lap. Desire curled in the pit of his stomach.

Whoa! he thought as he shook his head to clear it and concentrated on the road ahead. He needed to keep his mind on his work. He had a job to do and he was getting paid well for it. Besides, after years of experience, he knew the truth. Strength and good looks didn't guarantee happiness. He was just unlovable. And one thing was sure, he didn't need to let anyone get in his way right now. With that in mind, K.C. refused to look at her again for a very long time.

Chapter 4

Jessie woke with a jolt. *Where was she?* She looked down at her hands manacled on her lap. It all came back. She was sitting in the front seat of a beat-up blue Chevy with a ruthless man next to her who thought she had run away from home. He's an idiot. How could she be a runaway at twenty-eight? It was almost funny, but she wasn't laughing.

Her first experience with terror had happened when she witnessed that poor man's murder. The second time was being abducted by this K.C. person. She glanced at the profile of the man who held her prisoner. Jessie had been so frightened when he'd grabbed and handcuffed her, she'd only seen someone big, strong, and menacing, someone who was a threat to her freedom.

She hadn't even had a chance to pick up her bag. They must be miles now from where she checked it at the bus station. If this stupid thug hadn't suddenly swooped down on her, she'd almost be to her dad's by now. She clenched her teeth and her jaw muscles tightened as she relived the humiliation and fear of her capture. Fury built in her—surged through her. *Why am I playing the victim?* She trembled. Her fist clenched and her usual control whirled away as she thought of what he was forcing her to do.

He looked her way, and she let it rip. "You overbearing, bungling, stupid, dork," she yelled. "This is kidnapping! I'm not running away!!"

Jessie glared at him. His eyes narrowed and his face grew red with anger.

"Dork? Did you call me a dork?" he fumed. "Listen, 'rich britches.' No one's called me a dork since I was a kid. I hated it then, and I really hate it now. I'm not about to take it from a spoiled, rich kid whose mother would pay fifty thousand to get her little girl back."

"Fifty thousand dollars?" Jessie gasped.

His eyes sparked fire, and he reached into the glove compartment with his right hand. "Yes, fifty thousand dollars! Now, if you don't keep quiet, I'm gonna tape your mouth shut!"

"Good grief! I'm twenty-eight years old! Why would anyone pay a fifty thousand dollars for a grown woman?"

K.C. brandished a roll of duct tape in her face, and Jessie gulped. Glaring at her, he dropped the tape between them and ran a hand through his curly brown hair. Then he shook his head in disgust. She heard him grumbling under his breath as he focused his attention back on the road. Jessie studied her new enemy. Every muscle in his body had hardened with the tension of his rage. His chin jutted forward in determination and continued anger. He was coiled so tight he might spring out of control. Her anger changed to fear. She pressed herself against the door, as far from him as possible.

Several more miles went by before she felt the tension leave the air. His body finally relaxed. Suddenly he sat up straight, slammed his foot on the brake, and with a screech of tires, he pulled into the breakdown lane and onto the stony edge of the berm. As he turned toward her, Jessie flattened herself tighter against the side of the car. *If only the door would swing open,* she thought, *I could at least run.*

"What's the matter with you?" came K.C.'s perplexed question. His anger had been replaced by exasperation.

"Don't you dare come near me," she spat.

"What do you mean?"

"Why'd you pull over? You're not going to…you wouldn't…Oh, Lord, please help me…"

He chuckled, then just as quickly, his anger returned.

"Not your kind of man, huh? Don't worry, I wouldn't even think of it. You're hardly my type, either," he drawled as he looked at her in disdain.

Her face flushed with warmth at the humiliation of his sneering rebuff.

"I suddenly realized you had a locker key. Do you have the diamond pendant stashed back in Red Fish at the bus station? I need to get that necklace and return it to your mother."

"I have a duffle bag there," she began in a calm controlled voice. Her voice began to rise. "Mrs. Spaulding is not my mother, and I don't have any necklace!" she finished, nearly screaming the words into his face.

K.C. whipped the car around so sharply, she was thrown against him and then back against the door. Her wrists chaffed in the cuffs, and now her shoulder hurt from hitting the door. He stomped hard on the accelerator, throwing dirt and stones everywhere and sending the car forward with a jerk. Silence filled the car as they headed back to the small town they'd left over two hours before.

Twenty miles outside Red Fish they passed a black Mercedes driving out from town. A shiver snaked through Jessie. The two men in it looked alarmingly familiar.

Chapter 5

K.C. pulled into the parking lot at the left of the bus station. He pulled out Jessie's locker key, fingering the cool hard metal gingerly.

"We can get this tiresome job over with as soon as I have the necklace," K.C. commented as he tucked the key back into his pocket.

Before he got out, he unlocked the handcuffs. Jessie sighed with relief. Her freedom was short. Scowling at her, he snapped one bracelet around the steering wheel while the other went back onto her left wrist.

"I'm not taking any chances, 'Miss Runaway.'" He smirked as he exited the car and headed into the station.

As soon as he disappeared, she unlatched her seat belt and opened her door. She let the belt dangle near the latch and then pulled the door back until it was barely ajar.

Five minutes later, K.C. was back with her purple duffel bag.

"Looks like you'd planned for more than just overnight with this overstuffed grape." He hefted her duffel into the back seat.

K.C. slid partway into his seat and unlocked the handcuff. Jessie threw open the door. Jerking her arm away from the steering wheel, she slipped out of the belt and swung her feet onto the curb in one smooth movement. Suddenly Jessie's body jerked to a stop in mid-air as she was pulled back into the seat, her head smacking against the door edge.

"Thought you could escape, huh?"

Jessie's eyes filled with tears as pain shot through her head, down her neck, and into her shoulders. She held her head, trying to stop its spinning. She'd almost made it. Wiping away her tears, she turned to see that "the bully" had a death grip on the waistband of her jeans. He grabbed both her wrists, capturing them once again in their metal prison. She felt a black hole of despair grip her. *Why won't he listen to me? This oaf who thinks he knows everything. He doesn't have an inkling of the truth.* She collapsed hopelessly into the seat. Her head ached, but she wasn't about to ask for an aspirin. As they once again drove north, her thoughts returned to the reason she had traveled by bus with her ridiculous purple duffel.

***

After safely slipping through the gate at the Spaulding Mansion, Jessie headed towards the police station to report what she had seen. Her hands shook on the steering wheel. The road in front of her was blurry as tears continued to well from the corners of her eyes. Jessie was almost to the station when she suddenly remembered the police officer she'd seen lounging in Mrs. Spaulding's living room. Pulling to the side of the road, she sat twisting the end of her hair between her fingers, trying to think of what to do next. She couldn't just walk in and say, "Hey, I just saw someone murdered!" She didn't know anyone there whom she could trust. How many corrupt cops were there in Mrs. Spaulding's employ? Going to the police was out of the question. Someone in the force knew perfectly well what had happened but sat back and watched. For all she knew, the whole police department was in on it.

All her life Jessie had known just what to do when it came time to making big decisions. Now she felt lost. She couldn't forget what she saw or let it pass as if nothing had happened. *But where should I turn? Who should I tell about the murder I've seen? Should I call the FBI?*

Home, that's were she needed to go. Home meant safety, security, and her telephone books, including one for the largest city near Everett. Home was where everything was familiar, and she would be in control again. Jessie drove as fast as the speed limit allowed to her apartment building, parking in her numbered spot out front.

Dashing up the stairs, thoughts whirled through her head. She would call the FBI. Then maybe she should visit her Dad. Dad didn't like surprises, but he would just have to accept this one. She would call in sick at school, pack a few bags, and head for her dad's in Tucson. It would give her time to forget what she had seen.

Now that she had a plan, she felt sure of herself again. Jessie called the school and left a message for the principal, saying she was called out of town on a family matter. Changing from her suit, she threw on her most comfortable jeans, her red t-shirt, and her favorite running shoes.

Pulling down her purple Vera Bradley duffel from the closet shelf, she tossed it on the bed and opened her dresser drawers. As the bag sat open on her bed she started pushing in clean lingerie, her floral print T-shirt, silky boxer pj's, cosmetic bag and curling iron. Piled next to her bag was an extra pair of jeans, a couple of her favorite tops and extra socks.

Time to check the phone book to see if the FBI really was listed. *Let's see*, she thought, *FBI.* She flipped through the business listings. *Not There! Maybe it's Federal Bureau Of Investigation.* There it was looking quite ordinary along with Federal Building and Maintenance and Federal Business Systems. She punched in the numbers and tucked the cordless receiver between her shoulder and ear.

"Federal Bureau of Investigation, New York Field Office. Please listen carefully as some of our numbers may have changed since you last called."

"I don't believe this," she muttered. "Do people call them often?" Sitting on the bed, she continued to shove her clothes into the duffel.

"If you know your parties extension, please dial it now."

"I wish I did," Jessie told the impassive voice.

"For crimes dealing with fraud, press 1, for missing persons press 2…."

Automated crime reporting had infected the FBI.

"For computer crimes, press 3, for homicides press 4, for drug related crimes, press 5…."

She dropped the sock in her hand and jabbed 4 on the phone.

"All agents are busy, please hold."

"Arrgh!" she waited, her mind in a jumble.

Suddenly all her thoughts came to a screeching halt. Where was her purse? She needed her identification and money. She dropped the phone and dashed into the living room. No purse! Where did she have it last? Back in the bedroom, her thoughts continued to race. She knew she had it when she had stopped at the mansion. She'd pushed it up on her shoulder as she had walked so confidently toward the house. She didn't remember it after her hurried exit to the car. Was it in the bushes in front of the house or in the summerhouse? Well, she wasn't about to go back to look for it now.

She picked up the phone to hear, "please continue to hold, an agent will be with you shortly."

She would just have to drive to the airport and try to get a standby flight to Tucson. Even though the purse was lost, she still had her checkbook; and could pay for her airline ticket. *Oh, no."* Her heart sank. *My driver's license was in my purse. I can't fly.* Shifting the phone to her other ear, she glanced at the top of her bureau for any loose change. That's when she saw it. Her Visa Card was peeking out from the pages of the *Northern*

Expressions catalog. She remembered now. She was going to call in an order for her sister Jenny's birthday but had gotten distracted. Whatever the distraction, she was thankful for it. The card would be so much easier to use than checks.

I'll have to drive to Tucson. I hope I don't get stopped without my license.

"Thank you for holding, your call is important to us so please do not hang up."

Jessie glanced into the mirror at the back of her bureau. She hardly recognized herself. Her face was tearstained, hair was flying in all directions, and her eyes were wide with fear and frustration. No time to fix her makeup now. She moved back and forth between closet and dresser, continuing her search for things to take. Fumbling in her sock drawer, she found her secret stash of emergency money. Slipping her fanny pack out of the bottom dresser drawer, she began loading up with money, card, throat lozenges, tissues, another lipstick, comb and small brush.

"Please continue to hold. The next available agent will be with you in a moment."

She went back to her bed, flung the fanny pack next to the duffel, and tucked in the sock she'd dropped on the bed more than ten minutes ago.

Jessie's neck was getting stiff so she switched ears, again. She started for the closet to pick up her red windbreak and matching hat when she heard car doors slam outside under her window. Pulling aside the curtain, she froze. Behind her car, two dark suited men were standing next to their black Mercedes. *Something tells me they aren't selling Girl Scout cookies.*

Jessie slammed the receiver back on the cradle with a growl. *Looks like I take a bus.* Snapping her fanny pack around her waist, she grabbed her coat, hat, and duffel bag, slipped out the door and down the back steps. Jessie let herself out the back door of the building just as she heard the men shuffling up the front stairs toward her apartment. She ran all the way to the bus station, bought a ticket for the next bus leaving Everett and snuck on before loading time was even called. On the bus she wrapped her trembling arms around her bag and scooted down into the seat so no one could see her from outside. Her few days since then had been without plan or thought. In a daze she rode one bus after another, sleeping on them, eating little and always being hounded by fear. Since they knew who she was, they would probably find out more. They might even know about her father in Tucson.

***

Riding in the silence of the car, she now had time to think of something more than running. It was her purse, of course, that had tipped them off. She realized that now. It had everything in it about her, including her address.

The approach of a black car brought Jessie out of her reverie. As it passed in the opposite lane, she scrunched down with her head turned just enough to watch as it went by. The figures of two men in the front seat sent gut wrenching fear deep into her soul.

Chapter 6

K.C. heard a gasp. He turned to see 'Miss Runaway' hunch down in her seat. What was wrong now? She was watching a passing car, a black Mercedes. *Was that the same one that passed them before?* Her face was pinched and white with fear. He recognized that look. She'd had the same look when he'd captured her. Eventually she pushed herself into a sitting position. Why would that black Mercedes upset her? *They certainly can't have anything to do with us*. He thought about dismissing the idea that someone might be following him. *I'm the hunter, not the hunted.*

"Uh, Mr. Avalon?"

She looked like a small, trapped animal.

"Yah, what is it?"

"Would you please listen to my side of the story?" she begged, "I'm not a wild animal, you know."

Damn! She was doing it again, reading my mind.

"I'm a person! Hear me out before you throw me into the clutches of Mrs. Spaulding."

He'd had others begging him to let them go. Something inside of him cringed to hear this young woman begging. *Am I such an ogre that she would need to beg for my attention?* He thought back on the last few hours and realized he had been acting a bit barbaric. *Well maybe not just a bit, maybe a lot.*

His defenses had been up after having talked with her mother. Mrs. Spaulding had made a point of describing her as a willful, selfish, and rebellious child. Looking her over again he realized how defenseless she seemed. *What was the word? Oh yah! That was it, vulnerable, most certainly vulnerable, but most definitely not a child.* He had to admit she sure didn't act like the spoiled rich kid Mrs. Spaulding described.

"Sure, go ahead. Tell me your side of the story," he relented. "It will help pass the time as we drive back to Everett."

With a sigh she began. "I am a history teacher at Inglweiss Academy in Everett." He sat relaxed at the wheel, listening attentively.

"I care about my students, and that's what got me into this mess." Jessie paused.

"Continue."

"I went to Michael Spaulding's home to see if I could talk to his mother, Mrs. Spaulding, about his school work. I overheard an argument inside. A man was being interrogated and threatened."

"Do you always listen at people's doors?"

"I didn't mean to. I discovered a window was open, that was how I heard everything so well."

"So you were peeping as well."

"Will you shut up and let me tell you what happened?"

"Ok, Ok, I'm listening."

"By that time, I was afraid if those inside discovered me, they wouldn't understand my accidentally overhearing them. When I heard them coming outside, I hid in a small summerhouse near the mansion."

"Convenient," he commented.

"Then – then the worst part happened."

She hesitated and he looked at her. Her eyes were glassy with tears.

"I saw them dragging this man by the summerhouse. They called him Edward. Then I heard a shot, and when I looked again, there was blood on his chest and he looked dead." She gulped and went on.

"I waited until I thought it was safe and hid behind trees and bushes until I could get away. But they found out I was there and came after me. I panicked and have been running ever since."

By this time the tears were freely coursing down her cheeks. As she fumbled for the tissues she had stuffed into her pocket, K.C. pulled out his large white handkerchief and thrust it under her nose. Grabbing it with her handcuffed hands, she blew her nose and dabbed at her wet eyes. With a shudder she ended her story with his coming out of nowhere and manhandling her into his car. She sat in silence, waiting.

"You tell a good story, Miss Overton." He was touched by the sincerity of her words and the passion in her voice. Those damn tears, though – did she have to cry? In the past, a woman's tears had fooled and humiliated him many times. He really wasn't sure if he should trust the genuineness of her tears. They could just as easily be faked or used as a tool to sway him.

"Please, at least call me Jessie," she said with a tentative smile, handing him back his handkerchief, her cuffs clanking together. "I was hoping you would see me as a person to be respected, rather than an animal to be hunted."

"Uh, sure. You can call me K.C." Her offering of peace surprised him. "That's K period C period, like initials."

"Do you believe me?" she asked.

"About seeing a murder? Well, as I said, it was a good story. And I've heard some first-class ones in my business."

"But it's true! You have to believe me!" Her voice was sharp with panic.

"I don't have to believe anyone, and, at this moment, I'm not sure which one is telling the truth, you or Mrs. Spaulding." She said nothing, and he found her staring ahead again with that lost look.

It would be a long while before they'd get to the Ohio border, let alone New York. He just wanted this case over with. Driving straight through seemed like a good idea.

K.C. noticed that she'd nodded off to sleep. The setting sun was streaking across the dashboard and lit her hair until it glowed. It looked so soft and smooth in spite of the rough handling he'd given her.

A strange uncomfortable feeling began to gnaw at him. *What was it?* A hot flush surged up his neck and into his face as he realized what it was – shame. She was right. He'd treated her like an animal.

Had he grown so insensitive to those around him that he would treat a woman like a wild beast? She looked so defenseless huddled in the seat next to him. *Should I believe her? Could there be any truth in what she's told me? More importantly, can I trust her at all?* He hadn't trusted a woman in a very long time.

Darkness enveloped them as he drove north on a secondary road. He turned on the radio to a talk show to help keep him awake. It droned on and on.

Suddenly, the car bumped and jerked over uneven ground and someone screamed. K.C. stomped on the brake, and they screeched to a stop at the edge of a field. Shoving the car into park, he turned off the engine.

"Are you all right?" he shook his head to clear it.

"I think…so. What happened?" Jessie's voice shook.

"I fell asleep. I need to get some coffee."

The glow of the dash clock said 9:30 p.m.

He didn't want to do it, but he knew they would have to find a place to stay overnight. *I need to sleep, but how can I make sure she doesn't get away?* He found the thought of handcuffing her to a bed or chair less than perfect.

"Stay put. I'm going to make sure we can get out."

K.C. walked around the car, checked the tires and looked for a smoother way out to the road.

He snapped himself back into his seat. *Thank goodness we had our seatbelts on,* he reflected.

"Is the car ok?"

"It seems to be all right. I'm going to look for a motel in the next town." He turned the key in the ignition. The purr of the engine was reassuring. Nothing was damaged. He pulled the car around and they made their somewhat less bumpy way back onto the road.

"We'll have to work out something. I need to get some sleep."

Five more miles down the road, they entered a small town. Ahead of them, K.C. saw a flashing vacancy sign at a motel. He drove under a portico and up to the office door. A landscaped area of yews and spring flowers in a long brick container along the driver's side shielded arrivals from the road. At this point he didn't care about what might lay ahead tomorrow. He needed sleep.

K.C. turned to Jessie. "Your cat naps might help you, but I'm exhausted."

Again he uncuffed her hands and this time attached them both to the steering wheel.

"I'm not about to run away in the middle of the night." She replied disgustedly. "Especially with my hands cuffed."

"I'm just making sure of that," he answered. Scowling, he noticed the red chafe marks on her smooth white skin.

K.C. was out of the car, into the office, and back in minutes. Stepping out from under the portico he looked up. The sliver of moon was within days of disappearing, making the stars even more brilliant in the dark sky. He slipped back into the driver's seat. Suddenly a flash of headlights blinded him, reflecting in his side mirror. He looked up, searching for the source. Zipping down the highway, past the motel, was a familiar black car.

Chapter 7

From the darkness of her prison, Jessie watched as the black car barreled past them. *Oh, no! They're getting closer. I'm trapped like a rabbit.* The cuffs held her securely to the steering wheel. She tugged at them in frustration.

K.C. slowly unlatched the cuffs and snapped them shut on her hands again, starting the car without a word. Driving around to the back of the motel, they stopped in the parking space in front of door 15.

She couldn't stand his silence, "Did you see it?"

"Did I see what?"

"The black car!"

"I saw a black car."

"It's the same one!" She had a hard time keeping her voice from shaking. "I know that car."

"Forget cars," K.C. said as he released her seat belt, got out, and came around to open her door.

"Let's make a deal." He looked down at her. "It's late and we need to get some sleep before we continue. If you promise not to run away, I'll not handcuff you to the bed."

Handcuff me to the bed? Would he actually do that? She was right. He was a cruel man. She was so exhausted she felt like weeping. Promising nothing, she held up her wrists. K.C. retrieved the key from his pocket and opened the handcuffs. Pocketing them, he reached for her hand to help her out.

"Ouch!" Pain shot up the arm of the hand he held. She gasped as pain shot through her other arm as well. Still she held back her tears. She'd not give him the satisfaction of seeing her cry again.

"I'm sorry," K.C. said softly, concern furrowing his brow. "You shouldn't have fought against them. Your wrists look like raw meat." His finger gently traced the red, raw ring on her skin.

Jessie cringed and snatched her hand away from him. Wincing she straightened her shoulders and turned her back on him, walking stiffly to the door. Anger boiled up inside of her. *He's a beast! He throws his weight around manhandling me, and then pretends he's concerned about my raw wrists.*

"You'll find out how wrong you are," she said icily, "and when you do, I'm going to charge you with kidnapping. You'll be spending the rest of your life in prison."

Ignoring her, K.C. grabbed Jessie's duffel and his forest green backpack from the car, opened the door, and shoved her inside.

"Wait a minute." She stopped short and slowly looked around. A table and chairs stood near the door with the usual dressers nearby, but there was only one bed. A king sized bed.

"Don't worry," K.C. assured her as he dropped the luggage on the floor. "I'm going to sack out in one of those chairs or maybe the floor, whichever is most comfortable." He eyed them both with distaste.

"You'll only need one pillow, I'll take these three." He tossed them onto a chair. "I'll take that spread too." He dragged the heavy spread onto the floor, bunching it against the wall.

Jessie stood in the middle of the room watching in a trance, as K.C. moved around the room. He passed close to her as he piled the bedspread into a mountain of brown and gold fabric. Shaking her head she refocused and saw the bathroom ahead of her. *Maybe it has a window. I can sneak away before he realizes it.*

"It's been a long time on the road," she declared as she edged away from K.C. and toward the bathroom door, disappearing inside and locking it. Jessie turned slowly, surveying the tiny room. There was no way out. The bathroom window was a small square made up of dirty opaque glass blocks. She was surrounded with the pungent smell of disinfectants.

Well, at least I can take a shower. She turned the hot water on in the stall. Jessie couldn't remember when she'd had the luxury of a shower in the last few days. *What would she put on*? Her duffel was still in the other room and she needed clean clothes. Jessie opened the bathroom door and saw "the beast," his back partly turned toward her, rummaging through her luggage and talking to himself.

"It's got to be here," she heard him mutter. Her fanny pack, hat and red windbreak lay on the floor where he'd thrown them from her duffel. He pulled out her shirts and jeans, tossing them on the floor to one side. Next came socks, cosmetic bag and curling iron. He slowed down when he reached her boxer pj's, gingerly tossing them toward the pile of clothes he had uncovered. She knew the only thing left would be her lingerie. He just rummaged through it without looking, feeling for something. He felt the sides and bottom of the bag. *What was he looking for?* He started to pick up some of her clothes, stuffing them back in the bag.

"Maybe she hid it somewhere at the bus station?" he muttered, as he leaned back on his heels, shaking his head, her pj's in his hand. He was so engrossed in his thoughts that he failed to see the steam pouring from the bathroom.

Enough was enough! "What do you think you're doing with my clothes?" she yelled at him, slamming the bathroom door, sending wisps of steam flying through the room. Jessie marched across the room swiping the boxer pj's from his left hand as he stood, caught like a kid with his hand in a cookie jar.

K.C.'s mouth hung open in astonishment. Blood rushed up his neck turning his face red with embarrassment. The look on his face defused her anger, and she started to laugh. Jessie stood in the middle of the floor laughing and laughing, pj's clutched in her hands, and holding her stomach. Very slowly her legs folded beneath her, and she collapsed onto the floor. Her fingers loosened on her pj's, and they dropped into her lap. Slowly, her laughter turned to sobs, deep wrenching sobs. She clasped her arms around her body, rocking back and forth frenetically.

"Don't! Please don't cry." She looked up and saw K.C. standing, helplessly staring at her. The next moment he was beside her, gathering her into his arms. Holding her like a baby, Jessie's head against his shoulder, he began to rock her gently, awkwardly patting her hair, until her sobs became less frequent and the trembling in her body began to calm. As her gulps for breath lessened, she became aware of the spicy aroma of his cologne and realized where she was. Crying had left Jessie limp. Shaking herself from his arms, she clutched her pj's, stood, and with as much dignity as she could muster, walked toward the bathroom and her waiting shower.

Chapter 8

K.C. sat on the floor stunned. In less than a day, this Jessie Overton had succeeded in humiliating him. He hadn't felt so helpless since he was in third grade. *How could someone I hardly know, make me feel so many conflicting feelings?* Yet, holding her trembling body in his arms had felt so right.

He jumped to his feet. *Enough! I'm letting her get to me.* His hand brushed his shirt. It was wet. *Oh! Right! Her tears.* He wanted nothing more than to get cleaned up and into his sweats. The splashing of the shower continued behind the closed bathroom door. He'd have to wait. Instead he pushed the two chairs into the open space between the bed and the door, turning them toward each other. Using the three pillows he'd confiscated, he made a mattress of sorts with two and used the third pillow for his head. He'd have to sleep curled up. *Oh, well. I guess the fifty thousand is worth some discomfort.* K.C. picked up the spread and folded it in half creating a simple sleeping bag. He stood back to survey his work. *It will have to do for now.* Turning to the window next to the door, he cranked it open allowing in the fresh night air.

The shower stopped. Flicking off the lights, K.C. quickly slipped into the lumpy makeshift bed curling his body into a fetal position to fit. His back was to the bathroom but he heard the door slowly open, he closed his eyes to give her privacy. All was silent. *What am I doing? She could sneak up behind me and conk me on the head.* As he turned over in the improvised bed, the chairs slid apart and he slowly fell between them and onto the floor.

He managed a quick look as she dashed to the bed. Her slight body in boxer pj's with damp hair hanging in tendrils about her face and chin was oddly appealing. That sensation stirred again in the pit of his stomach, only now it was uncurling into something stronger. *What's the matter with me?* K. C. thought chagrined.

K.C. kicked away the spread and pushed himself into a sitting position. He felt grit from the floor beneath his hands and snorted in disgust. Getting up, he rubbed the dirt from his hands and quietly pulled the chairs together again. This time K.C. lay with his feet hanging out the back of the seat where wind from the window blew onto them, chilling him. Pulling the spread tighter around him, exhaustion finally won. *My shower can wait* was his final thought.

Chapter 9

Jessie never even glanced at K.C. as she ran barefoot from the bathroom. The big king size bed beckoned as an island of safety and comfort, even though she was still a captive of "The Dork." She quickly slipped between the sheets pulling the blanket up to her chin. As soon as her head hit the pillow she was asleep.

She always dreamed. This night the dream began pleasantly. She was walking through a beautiful meadow surrounded by three rollicking lambs and brilliant red poppies. The poppies' deep brown centers were like faces in red sunbonnets dancing back and forth, and the lambs played around them and around her feet. As she watched, the poppies began to change subtly. The brown centers grew larger and for a brief second the brown disappeared and reappeared in a blink. Each poppy had become an eye. They weren't dancing now but were watching her. She and the lambs turned to the left and the eyes followed her, hundreds of brown eyes, blinking and staring at her. She couldn't get away from their gaze. She ran, her mouth open in a bleating scream.

With a gasp she sat up, fear coursing through her. Her mind was in turmoil. Then, one question surfaced through the morass of emotion.

What am I doing...going like a lamb to slaughter? Her exhaustion had been temporarily satisfied and was now replaced by determination.

Slipping quietly from beneath the covers, she crawled to where her shoes and clothes lay on the floor next to her duffle bag. She slowly stood and turned hopefully toward the door, her escape route. *Oh, no. My only way out is blocked.* Breathing deeply and snoring lightly in sleep, her nemesis lay right in front of the door.

Didn't he trust her? She grimaced as she thought of the unspoken promise she'd sort of made not to escape. Here she was, trying to do just that. He wasn't taking any chances.

Jessie couldn't step over him to the door. That left the large window to the right of the door. At least it was open, but it was on the other side of the bed and close to where his feet lay on the chair seat.

Trying to slip through a window in boxer pj's sounded dangerous as well. She slipped her jeans and shirt on over her pj's, quietly stuffed her fanny pack and jacket back into the duffle and carefully lifted the duffle onto the bed. *Don't be stupid. Leave everything,* a part of her chided. *No Way. I'm not about to leave my only clothes behind,* she answered as she slowly shoved the duffle ahead of her. She started to crawl cautiously across the bed toward the window on the other side. Push…creep…push…creep. The king sized bed seemed to go on for miles. Finally she slipped over the edge, lifting her bag quietly to the floor.

Finding the latch on the screen, she pried it gently. Squeak…grind. To her, the squeaks were extremely loud, even though only squeaks. As the screen released, she stiffened and held her breath listening. There wasn't a sound.

She lowered the screen to the floor, picked up her bag and slid it through the narrow opening. Leaning out the window to drop the duffle softly to the ground, Jessie followed it with her head and arms.

Suddenly she couldn't move, stuck half in and half out of the window. Something gripped her by the waist, held her immobile, and then started to squeeze. *Did the window slide down? She had to get loose. She had to get out!* She pressed her hands against the shingles outside, pushing in panic to leverage herself through. With a yelp of surprise, her hands slipped from the siding as she found herself roughly dragged back into the room by two powerful hands and thrown onto the bed.

"You said I could trust you," K.C. spat as he stood over her, his face purple with anger. His fists were clenched at his sides. She watched him struggle for control. *Was he going to hurt her?*

"I…I didn't actually say it," she whispered as she lay trembling beneath his glare.

"You asked for it." Grabbing his handcuffs off the floor, K.C. captured her left wrist and attached it to the headboard.

"Hey! You can't do that!"

"I just did."

K.C. reached over the windowsill and pulled her duffle back inside, throwing it onto the bed where it landed on Jessie's legs. *Dork…bully…madman,* she fumed inside as she kicked the bag out of her way. She had been so close to getting away, what had gone wrong? Of course, she should have realized. The silence before she slipped the screen to the floor should have warned her. The deep breathing and snoring had stopped. The grinding and screeching must have wakened him.

Jessie lay fully clothed and sleepless trying to find a comfortable position. In the early morning hours, she finally slipped into a restless doze.

Chapter 10

Jessie slowly opened her eyes and uncurled her body. Why was her left arm so stiff? She swung her right arm out from her side. It landed on something warm and soft. She looked at the warm thing her arm rested on and saw K.C., sprawled on his back on top of the covers. Suddenly she remembered her unsuccessful attempt to escape. Her left arm ached. She quietly lifted her right arm, pushed herself up and away from her tormentor and huddled against the headboard so she could bend her left arm and rub it.

K.C. groaned in his sleep and threw his arms out, then crossed them on his chest, holding onto each arm until his knuckles were white. Jessie held her breath and didn't move, watching him. His face twisted in fright as he dreamed. She stared at this six-foot man who had been terrorizing her. In sleep, he looked like a frightened child.

If only she could get up and away while he slept so soundly. She might have gotten away this morning, but her aborted attempt last night prevented that possibility. She pulled on the handcuffs, but only succeeded in hurting her wrist and jiggling the bed. The movement woke K.C. He slowly opened his eyes and looked right at her. She turned her back on him and pressed herself against the headboard.

"Sorry I had to get rough with you last night," he said, propping himself up on one arm. "I can't afford to let you get away."

He rolled off the bed, grabbed his backpack and headed for the bathroom. She glared at his retreating back. Soon she heard the sound of the shower – and something else – he was singing?

How dare he sound happy! Here she was stuck to the bed with an aching arm and that beast was acting like he's on stage. She seethed with anger. He reentered the room grinning, dressed to go on the road again. He knelt down beside her. The spicy fragrance she'd noticed earlier enveloped them both. Her body tensed as he took out the key and unlocked the handcuffs first from the bed and then from her wrist.

"You egotistical, unfeeling monster." She beat on his chest with her fists.

Catching her hands in his, he lifted her until she was standing on the floor, shaking in front of him, the bedcovers lying in a pool of fabric at her feet.

"I'll wait outside while you freshen up." He released her abruptly and she fell back onto the bed. "No more sneaking out. I'll be watching." Turning, he shouldered his backpack and was out the door.

All she could think of was another hot shower to help heal her stiff muscles. Steam again filled the small bathroom as she stepped under the pulsing cascade that flowed from the showerhead. Her whole body relaxed from the heat as the hot water rolled across her shoulders and neck. She flexed her arm. It was losing most of its stiffness. Her anger ebbed. She was ready to confront her nemesis once again. Dressing quickly, she slipped on her windbreak and hat taking one last look in the mirror as she headed for the door. Color had returned to her cheeks. A fringe of bangs peeked out from the visor of the cap that framed her face, and her ash blond hair brushed the sides of her chin. *There is no sneaking away now*, she told her reflection. He would be watching her.

The morning air was brisk, carrying with it an exciting hint of warmth and freshness that only comes in spring. A breeze swept her hair across her face and gave her spirits a boost. Then she saw K.C. He was turning toward her, reaching to take her duffel to toss with his pack in the back of the car. His forehead was drawn together in a deep frown. All earlier cheerfulness was gone.

"OK, where did you stash it?"

"Stash what?"

"The necklace. Tell…me…where it is…now!" He was towering over her, his hands on his hips.

"You searched me, you searched my bag, and you found nothing!" *I can play this game too.* She stood, hands on her hips, glaring right back at him. "Can't you see I'm telling you the truth? I am who I told you I am. I'm not related in any way to Mrs. Spaulding."

She turned sharply and slid onto the seat as he held her door open. She was thoroughly disgusted. What would it take to convince him? As he got into the car, she held out her arms toward him, waiting for the expected lockup.

"You're on probation," he said looking at her reddened wrists. "If you give me any more trouble – well, you know what to expect."

Jessie lowered her arms and snapped herself with the seat belt.

"Have you thought about what I told you? No necklace should be proof." *How many times did she have to plead with him?* "You're condemning me to death if you take me to Mrs. Spaulding. I witnessed a murder. Just because she told you I was her runaway daughter, doesn't mean that she was telling the truth."

K.C. looked straight into her eyes. She stared right back at him. He looked wary. She could almost see him weighing the financial security that this job would give him against the possible injustice if she were right.

"Let's say you're telling me the truth," he said. "I want to be sure. I won't take you directly back to Mrs. Spaulding. Instead, I'll look into your story a little more before I do. But there's a condition. You have to stay at my apartment, and you can't try to run away. If you're telling the truth, that shouldn't be a problem."

Jessie's breath came out in a whoosh. She hadn't realized she had been holding it.

"Yes! Yes! I agree," she cried. For the first time in days she felt a sense of hope.

"The clerk told me of a local restaurant that serves breakfast." K.C. started the car. "Are you hungry?"

"Starved," she replied, thankful that there were no handcuffs and they were on a safe subject.

"Who pays?" she asked. "I don't have any cash."

"Don't worry, it comes out of my expenses."

Jessie loved breakfast. She hadn't had a decent one since she ran out of her apartment. Her whole family used to eat big breakfasts and lunches and then skimped on supper. That was one of the ways she was able to keep her weight down. She never changed that habit, even now when she was on her own.

Half a mile down the road they saw a sign for The Egg and I Family Restaurant. The oblong brick building was unimpressive except for the parking lot that was jammed with cars. Apparently this was the place to find the best breakfasts.

The bell over the door jangled as they entered, and, in spite of the overcrowded lot, a smiling waitress found them a table for two near the kitchen. Smells of bacon, toast, and coffee permeated the air.

She would have asked for help from the waitress if she hadn't made that bargain with K.C. She couldn't count on the Everett police with a traitor in their midst. This inept private investigator might be her next best help. Besides, he was buying breakfast, and she was starved. She opened the menu and scanned the many selections and their tempting colorful pictures. The farmer's breakfast caught her eye, but she decided to be reasonable. Not having eaten well since she was on the run, she didn't want to get sick by overindulging.

Jessie's mother had taught them not to live by chance. They could take control and make good choices for themselves like eating healthy. She frowned. Lately her whole life seemed to be out of her control. At least she could make a good choice now. She finally settled for a Western Omelet, a large glass of orange juice, dry wheat toast with homemade strawberry jam, and home fries.

K.C. watched as she attacked her meal.

"You enjoying that omelet?"

"I haven't eaten this well in weeks. You seem to be indulging in quite a feast yourself," she countered as she eyed his triple stack of pancakes, steak, and home fries. "That should keep you going for a while."

"I always like to eat well when I'm on a case. I figure I need lots of energy."

"Bringing in defenseless women?"

"You're hardly defenseless."

"Miss," he called to the waitress, "could you bring me another cup of black coffee?"

"That's your third cup," Jessie pointed out.

"Is that a problem? Sometimes I need even more to get wired for the day."

Pointing to her empty plate he continued, "I've never seen a woman who could put away such a large breakfast so fast."

Jessie grimaced as she put down her fork and finished her juice.

"If you're ready, we'd better get going," he said gruffly. "If we make good time, we'll reach Everett by late tomorrow night."

The tension and weight of the conflict between them had lessened somewhat with their bargain. As K.C. turned the car onto Interstate 70, they again fell silent.

At least he's heard me, she thought, whether he completely believes my story or not. That's got to count for something.

Jessie was shaken by the thought of how suddenly the ordinary can be shattered when something evil and unexpected happens. Witnessing a murder, being hunted and threatened just doesn't happen in her ordinary world. Jessie had never thought about being safe. She just felt she was.

At least K.C. was going to give her a chance to prove her story. *Will I ever feel safe with this man?* He actually smiled when they made their bargain earlier, a rather enticing smile at that, with a deep dimple in his chin. She hadn't seen a dimple like that since the old Kirk Douglas movies she enjoyed watching.

Jessie studied him as he drove. K.C. could definitely be the "body building" poster for any of the local gyms. In spite of his rudeness, she suspected there was a tender aspect to this man, but he kept it hidden. Hadn't he held her when she cried? Now that she thought about it, the incident was like a big brother comforting his little sister. She'd never had a big brother. Was that what she wanted, a big brother who could make everything right again? What would it take to break through his tough act? He was so opposite from anyone she'd ever known – especially Jeff.

Chapter 11

As they rode in silence through the countryside, K.C. thought about what Jessie had told him. He could feel her watching him. *What can she be thinking?* He wanted to believe her, yet so many times women had deceived him.

It had taken quite a few heartbreaks for him to realize that women used him as a trophy date. When he looked for a serious relationship, K.C.'s hard won muscles betrayed him, leaving him uncertain and wondering if he was only liked for his body. Commitment on his part became harder to make. So far not one of his past relationships had been satisfying.

Then, he thought, *there was the money.* All his financial problems would be solved with what he'd receive from this case. He had to admit, he'd been puzzled when Mrs. Spaulding offered him more than his usual fee. *Well, hey, who was he to question a gift of that magnitude falling into his lap?* Now it made him wonder again. K.C. glanced at his feisty captive and finally broke the silence.

"You say your mother is dead. Do you have other family?"

She looked at him in surprise. "My father lives in Tucson. He and Mom retired there and were planning on a long quiet time together." Her voice faltered. "Then Mom became sick."

"Any sisters or brothers?"

"A sister, Jennifer Lynn. She's three years younger than I and happily married with a new baby in California." There was a catch in her voice as she answered.

K.C. kept one eye on his driving as he watched Jessie twisting her hair around her fingers. Her eyes glistened with unshed tears. *Was it her mother's illness that made her so sad?*

"So there's no family here who can verify your story," he mused out loud.

She gave him a sharp look. K.C. focused on the road.

"What about you? Any family?"

K.C. frowned as he thought of his family.

"No one now," he replied angrily. He saw her frown. "Sorry, I didn't mean to snap at you."

"Not even brothers or sisters?" she pushed, ignoring his anger and apology.

"I'm an only child."

"So your parents are dead."

"Not exactly."

"Not exactly? How can someone be not exactly dead?" She persisted.

K.C. frowned. He was getting fed up with her badgering.

"You sure are nosey!"

"Sorry. None of my business." She turned abruptly away from him.

Who was the captive here, anyway?

For a short time they rode in silence.

"They just weren't there," he found himself saying in a voice husky with emotion.

She looked at him sideways. He could feel her eyes staring at him.

"I was pretty much on my own most of my life," he continued, keeping his eyes averted and concentrating on the road. "My real Mom died when I was six. When Dad remarried, he and my stepmother were too busy working or traveling together to think about a skinny insecure kid. I was just excess baggage."

She sat in silence. He could see her fingers twirling the ends of her hair, her sad eyes watching him. Embarrassed by his candor, K.C. looked away and then down at the dashboard. What he saw brought him up short. *Oh, no. I don't need this.*

K.C. pulled off at the next exit and onto the side of a country road. "Don't move. I have to check on the engine."

He tripped the hood, lifting it effortlessly. He gingerly loosened the radiator cap with an old greasy rag and checked on the water. It was nearly empty. He slammed the lid and got back in the car. When he started the car, he rolled down the windows, put the heat on high and turned on the fan.

"What are you doing?"

"The car is overheating," he told her.

"Has this happened before?"

"Naw…chasing you around the countryside used up the water in the radiator," he answered sarcastically.

"Right, it's all my fault," Jessie grouched.

"Look – we may have a leak. Meanwhile, I've heard if you run the heater, it will keep the temperature down on the engine."

"But it's so hot."

"It's the only thing we can do until we find a service station and get it fixed. Otherwise, we'll be stuck out here."

K.C. stripped off his body hugging T-shirt, tossing it in the back seat. "You might want to take off your hat and jacket. This could become a very hot ride."

He noticed her sneaking a quick look at his already sweat glistening chest.

They began their trip again, windows open, heat blowing, and Jessie dripping.

"I'm roasting," she gasped. "At least you can go without a shirt."

"So can you if you want," he said with a grin. "I won't stop you."

With a decided snort, Jessie folded her arms in front of her, but not before he caught her admiring the tight muscles across his chest and abdomen. *What would the touch of her fingertips feel like on his body?* K.C. was startled and disturbed by the thought. He quickly looked away.

"Look, there's a sign for a truck stop," she called out. "Three more miles."

Three miles seemed forever when driving in a sauna. Relieved, K.C. pulled into the gas station of the truck stop, pulled on his shirt, and hopped out to talk to the attendant.

"We're in luck," he told Jessie. "He says it's probably a leak in the water hose and he can have it fixed in forty-five minutes. The restaurant here looks good. Maybe we should get some lunch while we're waiting."

"Sounds good to me," she agreed as she undid her seat belt and stepped out of the car. "I need to cool down."

"Don't forget our bargain," he reminded her. "No running away."

"And, *you* treat me with more dignity!" she retorted.

The restaurant was decorated like the 50's with posters of Elvis and other rock and roll stars. Maroon Naugahyde booths lined the walls. There was a counter straight out of an old drugstore ice cream parlor, and tables with bent wire chairs filled the center of the room. The smell of hamburgers and french fries wafted through the air. K.C. led Jessie to a corner booth near the kitchen at the back of the room.

"Hi there, folks. What'll it be?" A waitress in a short apron and even shorter dress stood waiting for their order.

"What are your specials?" Jessie asked.

"Well, we have homemade chicken noodle soup, Jake's meatloaf dinner, and apple pie a-la-mode," she answered.

"I'll take it."

K.C. looked at her in disbelief.

"Well, I'm hungry! You forget I haven't eaten much for a long time."

"I think you're just taking advantage of my paying the bills." He smiled and shook his head. K.C. looked at the waitress and ordered the same. Soon they were enjoying a companionable lunch, finding it easy to chat about the décor and food as they ate. While waiting for their dessert, the conversation grew personal again.

"It must have been hard growing up," she ventured.

"Yah! It was," he answered. "Since I was a skinny runt, the bigger guys made it a point to keep me in line. Most of the time no one was at home for me to turn to except the babysitter, and she wasn't much help. In the long run I did all right. Once I'd reached a growth spurt, I made sure no one picked on me again. I did have one good friend, but mostly I learned not to depend on anyone but myself!"

K.C.'s words echoed in his ears. What a lonely sounding boast it seemed.

"Sounds like you've gone through a few losses yourself," he said, changing the subject.

She looked at him and K.C. found himself gazing into eyes saddened by some unknown pain. She seemed to swallow a lump in her throat. Suddenly the words gushed out in a tangle of emotions.

"Our family was so close. Suddenly everything fell apart. First Jennie got married and moved. Then Dad and Mom moved, and I lost Mom. And, and…" her voice slid away, and tears again welled in her eyes. Unconsciously, she twisted her hair through her fingers.

"What is it?" he asked. *Dare he touch her?* He tentatively covered her free hand on the table with his own large fingers.

“Ever since my family went in different directions, I’ve been so lonely,” she confessed with a sob.

“Here ya go, folks. Here’s your apple pie a-la-mode,” the waitress’s cheery voice broke in.

Jessie pulled her hand back, reaching for a tissue to dab at her eyes. K.C. was silent as he concentrated on eating his dessert.

When the last of the pie and ice cream had been consumed, he smiled at Jessie, picked up the check, and jostled his way through the tables to pay the bill at the register. As he reached for his change, he glanced out the window behind the cashier. A black Mercedes was pulling into the parking lot.

Chapter 12

Jessie watched K.C. bump into a nearby table, apologize to the customers, and then weave his way between tables to the cashier. He towered over those around him, his snug shirt outlining his muscles with every move. His progress didn't go unnoticed. Women at the table in front of Jessie whispered to each other as they watched K.C. make his way to the register.

One young woman fanned herself with her menu, commenting, "Now there goes six feet of gorgeous muscle!" The others added their approval.

"Hands off, ladies," Jessie muttered when she heard them. *Now what made her say that?* She looked back as K.C. was reaching for his change. He looked up, and then suddenly stepped back from the cashier and into an alcove. *That's strange.*

Jessie saw a sign pointing to restrooms where K.C. was standing. That wasn't so unusual, but she noticed that he didn't go into the men's room. He hovered quietly behind a rack of postcards and a shelf of souvenirs.

What is going on? His actions made her nervous. She leaned back against the booth. Raised voices drew her attention back to the front in time to see two men in dark suits and sunglasses pushing their way through the entrance. The doors crashed against the wall.

"Oh…no!" Jessie gasped in horror. They were the same men she'd seen kill Edward – the same ones at her apartment front door. Her heart thumped wildly. *I've got to get out of here!*

As the men slowly surveyed the room, Jessie slid under the table. She peeked around the table's edge trembling with fright. *Thank you, Lord! They're not looking this way.* Jessie scooted quickly across the sticky floor toward the kitchen's swinging door next to the booth. She slipped silently through it, looking anxiously around the busy kitchen for escape.

"Help me! Do you have a back door?"

"Back that way, Miss," replied a nearby cook, pointing over his shoulder to a door nearly hidden by boxes of produce and cans.

Jessie ran for the door, stumbling over a box of apples as she pushed her way through and around reeking trash bags. Her only thought was to get as far away as possible. Running to the right side of the building, she looked anxiously around the parking lot. Cars and people were everywhere. Where could she go?

She turned back toward the building and saw trees behind the dumpster just beyond the left side of the restaurant. She dashed to the side of the huge metal contraption, and was instantly overwhelmed with the sweet smell of rotting garbage. Behind the reeking receptacle there was a jumble of trees, bushes and tangled grape vines. She picked her way through the weeds and found what she needed – a place to hide. Jessie ran headlong through the brush to the edge of an embankment, down a short hill into the first line of trees. At first, the trees were sparse and far apart with little undergrowth, but soon both trees and brush became denser. Sharp bull briar thorns tore at her jeans and arms, making painful red lines on her skin. She wished now that she had her jacket and hat to protect her from scratches. Sapling branches whacked against her body as she ran. The light dimmed as she crashed deeper into the forest. *Do they see me? Are they following?* Jessie pushed through the undergrowth. Blood oozed across her arms and face. Still, her fear drove her on. The dense brush impeded her as well as giving her a sense of protection. No one could see her now, she was sure, although she realized her crashing through the woods was making unbelievable noise. *Am I safe? Do I dare look?* Jessie glanced over her shoulder to see if she was being followed. Suddenly her feet were treading air as the ground dropped out from under her. With a startled scream she fell in a shower of dirt and rocks, landing with a thud. Her head bounced painfully against something hard and the world around her faded into oblivion.

Chapter 13

K.C. flattened himself against the restroom doorway and watched. One of the men stepped forward, carefully scanning the people in the restaurant. The other gave the waiting hostess a flick of dismissal with one hand as he joined his partner in peering at the patrons. Customers gradually became aware of the black suited men and watched nervously as the threatening pair circled the room.

K.C. recognized one of the men from his visit to the Spaulding house. It was hard to tell them apart, but the man with jagged scar on the side of his face had let him into the home. A bulge, prominent under each man's tightly buttoned black coat, had to be guns.

He knew in his bones that they were looking for Jessie. She was telling the truth. A jolt of fear surged through him. Jessie! He anxiously looked for her in their corner booth. It was empty. As the men finished their circuit of the room, K.C. stepped from the doorway to confront them. The men glared at K.C with unconcealed menace. Then scarface smiled knowingly, shoving him aside as they exited the restaurant. *They know who I am. They've been following me all along. I'm supposed to be the hunter not the hunted.* The situation brought back feelings of helplessness he'd hoped were gone.

His next thought brought him back to the present with a jolt. *These men weren't here to bring back a rebellious runaway daughter. They were here to make a more permanent arrangement.*

Where's Jessie? He would have seen her if she'd gone by him to the restrooms. He watched as the men entered their car, but they didn't drive away. The two men sat watching the front door, waiting for K.C.'s next move. *Are they even sure Jessie is with me*, he wondered? They must have seen two people in the car as they passed us those times on the highway. Or did they?

K.C. stepped away from the window area and slowly moved to the back booth. Jessie's napkin lay on the floor halfway to the kitchen. K.C. pushed the swinging door open where he was assailed by moist warm air and the smell of cooked onions, coffee and meat.

"Did a pretty girl come this way?"

Without looking up from the meatloaf he was making, the nearest cook pointed to the back door. Cautiously he slipped out the door hugging the back wall of the restaurant, and moved to the edge of the building. He looked carefully around the corner to the parking lot. The Mercedes sat directly in front of the door and the men sat poised and alert within.

It wouldn't take them long to realize he'd left by a different way. K.C. knew what to do. His tracking skills were honed from years of following Roger at school and from these past years on the job. It didn't take him long to find trampled brush and some broken twigs on the bushes near the woods behind the dumpster. He carefully followed the trail of crushed undergrowth Jessie unintentionally left behind. He didn't dare call out to her in case the men left their car and heard him. Deeper into the woods he moved. He noticed a footprint in the soft earth, leaves kicked up and branches broken on the low bush blueberries. His slow progress saved him from sure disaster when suddenly before him he saw the ragged edge of a broken cliff. Exposed rocks and scuffed dirt at his feet were sure signs of someone having recently slid off the edge.

"Jessie?" he called softly. "Jessie, are you there?"

Silence. He cautiously moved to the edge of the cliff. As he started to look over, his stomach twisted violently and sweat broke out on his forehead. Stumbling back, he physically threw himself away from the cliff edge and leaned against the trunk of a massive maple as dizziness threatened to overwhelm him.

"No!" he gasped, "Please not that!"

Why now? Why here? He'd been so careful to avoid anything that put him into these kinds of situations. He'd almost forgotten the gut wrenching panic it caused him. But what could he do now? K.C. was in a situation that couldn't be avoided. He wasn't about to leave Jessie here, knowing the dangerous threat behind them.

He moved to the edge again, leaning slowly forward. The dizziness threatened again and his palms grew clammy as his body shook. Again he had to pull back in panic. He couldn't do it. At least not standing. Swiftly K.C. dropped to the ground, slithered around until he was on his stomach with his head facing the edge of the cliff.

He slowly pulled himself over the leaf-strewn ground toward the lip of the cliff. The solidness of the earth helped him feel secure and kept his head from swimming. K.C.'s fingers reached the cliff edge and dug into the soft crumbling dirt. He gently pulled himself forward, his eyes squeezed tightly shut. He opened them slowly and saw treetops twenty feet below him. On an outcrop of rock and dirt, half way down the cliff, lay the inert body of Jessie. She was being held in place by a scraggly white pine that was growing on the outside edge of the rock. It's gnarled roots twisted around and into stony crevices across the edge of the ledge. She was covered with dirt and tiny pebbles. Where her head lay on the rock, a small pool of blood had formed.

If she should suddenly awaken, K.C. thought, *she might unknowingly roll off the rock. What should I do?* Below him was Jessie. In front of the restaurant were two armed men who would soon be searching for them. And here he was between them, petrified by a lifetime fear that had him immobilized.

Chapter 14

Jessie's head pulsated with pain as it kept rhythm with her heartbeat. The throb grew into one fierce ache that radiated throughout her body. She was afraid the pain would get worse if she moved or opened her eyes, so she lay still. *What happened? Why do I hurt so much?* Something seemed to be wrong with her hearing also. Was there a snake nearby? She thought she heard it hissing. It rose and fell on waves of pain. "s..s..ie!" "e..s..s..ie!"

She groaned and turned her head side-to-side trying to get away from the hissing. The pain sharpened and shot through her as she did, bringing her close to the edge of unconsciousness again. She abruptly stopped and tried to lie as still as possible.

There was that snake again. The hissing formed into words and took shape in her mind.

"J..e..sssie don't move!" The voice seemed familiar.

Her eyes flicked open. The flash of light sent waves of pain through her head forcing her to shut them again. She gasped. *I was afraid of that. Keep your eyes closed* she chided herself.

"Jessie! Don't move! You'll fall off the ledge!"

This time she slowly opened her eyes. Despite the canopy of leaves above her, the world seemed to shimmer with light. Squinting against the brightness, she clenched her jaws against the pain until she could tolerate it. Wavering high above her was a face. Its twisted features were nearly unrecognizable. She tried moving her right hand and arm. Nothing seemed broken. Her hand moved automatically to her head. *Ouch!* She pulled her hand back and looked at it – blood. She slowly reached out to the right, away from her body, until she felt a wall of dry crumbling dirt and stone. She then moved her left hand and felt sharp stones, gritty dirt, something hard – then nothing but air. She pulled her hand back until she felt something solid. Painfully turning her head left she saw a bent and twisted white pine, her fingers rested on one of the tree roots that had pushed into the tiny cracks of the stone she was lying upon. Beyond that she saw the tops of pine trees dancing in the wind. The face above her had now come into focus and she recognized K.C. But why was he just lying there looking down?

"Help me," her mouth formed the words but they came out only as a whisper. She tried to inch herself up on her elbows, but she didn't have the strength. As she fought waves of pain, her arms gave way and she fell back onto the hard surface. Closing her eyes, she tried again, slowly, carefully, pushing herself upward. The weakness wasn't so overwhelming this time. She gradually pushed up on her elbows until the palms of her hands supported her. She stopped to rest, then pushed up as high as she could and slid her hips under her so she was in a sitting position.

Jessie carefully turned and leaned her back against the sloping dirt wall. Debris and dirt fell into her hair and over her body. She coughed and closed her eyes against the dust as her head whirled from the effort. When she opened her eyes again, she saw the precarious position she was in. She was sitting on a rock outcropping about three feet wide that made an island of safety in an otherwise sheer drop. If she had fallen a few inches more either way, she would no doubt have died, ending up on the ground or treetops below. She began to shake.

"K.C., help…me!" she begged, her voice stronger now but still wavering as she looked up at him.

K.C.'s face was white with fear. She knew from his distorted features that it wasn't just her predicament that caused him distress. He was frozen in a personal fear that she didn't understand.

Sudden awareness animated K.C.'s face, as if he awakened from the depths of a terrifying dream. He gasped, "I'll try." Slithering slowly on his stomach away from the edge of the cliff, he disappeared.

"K.C.?" Jessie's voice rose in panic. "Are…you…there?" Her voice shook. "K.C. I'm scared, don't leave me."

"I'm here, Jessie," he replied "I can't find anything to let down to you." He sounded helpless and confused.

"Is…there…anything at the gas station?"

"Those men that scared you off are waiting for us there. I expect them to show up any minute."

What are we going to do? Jessie slumped in discouragement.

"Jessie, can you stand up and lift your arms up over your head? I need to see how far you are from the cliff edge. Maybe I can grasp your arms."

Jessie started to push herself up, pressing her back against the rocky cliff side. She kept the edge of the ledge in view so she wouldn't accidentally step off. Inch by inch she slid up, pebbles and dirt spilling down around her feet as her back dislodged them. Small stones crunched unevenly under her feet as she shifted her weight. Finally she was standing. A wave of dizziness swept over her. Her fingers gripped the stone and dirt wall behind her as she steadied herself. Jessie kept her eyes straight ahead and tried not to look over the edge of her island of safety. Slowly she reached up. Tilting her aching head upward, she looked for K.C.

He was again flat on the ground. With his face barely over the cliff, she could see he was trembling. Sweat beaded across his forehead. Her fingertips came about two feet below where he lay. He would have to scoot forward enough to let his arms dangle over the edge of the precipice. She watched as he slithered forward. It looked like his eyes were closed as he moved into position.

K.C.'s arms snaked slowly down toward her. Another look confirmed that his eyes were tightly shut. What she feared was confirmed. The muscle bound hulk of a man was petrified of heights. She stretched her arms even higher toward his extended hands.

"This isn't going to work," she cried. Tears of frustration welled up in her eyes.

K.C.'s eyes flew open, and he saw that his fingertips barely brushed hers. To lift her, he would have to grip her wrists and she his.

"I'll have to move a little further. Jessie, turn and face the cliff. When you feel my hands grasping your wrists, hold tight to mine. As I pull, use your feet to climb up the cliff."

Jessie saw his body tense as he slid a little further out over the edge. His eyes widened as he strained to keep them open.

She slowly turned to face the cliff. The smell of rotting leaves and earth filled her nostrils. Suddenly she felt the rock slip and shift beneath her feet.

"K.C.!" she screamed, "the ledge is moving. "I'm too heavy for it."

"Quick. Up on your tiptoes!"

Jessie inched up on her toes, reaching as far as she could. She closed her eyes as another sickening wave of dizziness gripped her. Dirt and stones trickled down on her as K.C. continued to lean forward and reach down. His hands slid slowly down to her wrists and grabbed hold. The ledge shifted again and tipped slightly down away from the cliff as her weight loosened the huge rock from its dirt anchor. With a gasp of fear, her fingers closed about his wrists. His skin was ice cold. His body shook.

Jessie's arms trembled as K.C. wiggled his body, trying to pull himself back and her up. *The toes of his shoes must be digging into the dirt behind him,* she thought as he shifted back and forth trying to inch his way back from the edge. Her arms stretched upward and a new pain like tiny needles pierced her already bruised arms and shoulders. Jessie's sneakers slid and pushed against the side of the cliff. Her island of safety shifted and bucked. There was a rattle of earth, her grip tightened on K.C.'s wrists, and suddenly her feet were thrashing in the air. A sharp crack split the air and another. Jessie looked down in time to see the ledge bouncing off the granite cliff and crashing into the treetops below her, disappearing from sight.

There was no turning back. Her feet scrabbled against the cliff. She felt herself being gradually lifted upward. Looking up, she realized he was now kneeling, and the muscles in his arms rippled with strain both physical and emotional. His face was red and the sweat that had beaded his forehead before now ran in rivulets down his cheeks. The closer she came to the cliff edge, the harder he pulled until he was squatting, leaning back from the edge – pulling. The sweat now poured from his face. The pain and strain on her arms was excruciating. As her shoulders topped the edge, he pulled back with one mighty lunge and her feet scrabbled up the last of the dirt wall.

With a crash, she was over the lip of the cliff. K.C. fell back onto the leafy soil with a thud, and she landed on top of him. His arms went limp at his sides. She lay spent on top of him, her arms on either side of his body, her hands resting in his. They lay there gasping and panting.

She slowly became aware of the sweaty hardness of his body under her. Her head lay on his chest, just under his chin. Jessie could hear his heart thumping like a runaway train. Her hands warmed his icy ones. She rolled off his body and onto her back with a shiver that had nothing to do with cold.

Lying on the musty ground, she could no longer hold back the tears. They slid from under her lids, down her face and into her hair. She was exhausted. Her head hurt, her body ached, and she was shaking with fear and strain. K.C. pushed himself up on one elbow and looked at her, then at the place from which she had just climbed. Deep furrows in the earth marked the path that his feet and legs had gouged in the effort that pulled her from certain death. Jessie watched as a look of astonishment spread across K.C.'s face.

Chapter 15

"K.C.?" Jessie slowly pushed herself up and reached out to him. "Are you all right?" Her hand tentatively brushed his arm.

"I…did…it," he marveled. He suddenly sat up, his eyes wide. "I really did it!"

Unexpectedly Jessie found herself crushed against his chest, his arms enfolding her.

"K.C.?" Jessie's muffled voice queried from the folds of his dirt-covered shirt. "You're afraid of heights, aren't you?"

Instantly he loosened his grip on her and pushed her away, holding her at arms length. *That was a stupid thing to say*, she chided herself. *Of course he was afraid of heights. He didn't want anyone to know, dummy! Now he'll be angry and take me back to Mrs. Spaulding.*

Jessie frowned as she watched K.C.'s face. He didn't look angry. His eyes searched hers. Would this macho guy actually admit he was frightened into immobility?

"What makes you think…"

Jessie felt a shudder run through his body, his eyes dropped, as did his arms.

"Yes…" he hesitated, "something terrifying happened to me as a kid."

"What was it?"

"I've never been able to go down a sliding board or swing on a swing since that time."

Before he could explain further there was the snap of a branch and rustling of bushes behind them. A low murmur of voices reached them.

Grabbing her hand, K.C. pulled Jessie to her feet and gestured for her to be quiet. They stumbled over roots and rocks as they pushed their way through the brush along the edge of the ridge away from voices. The further they went, the faster K.C. walked. His long strides would have left her behind had he not been gripping tightly to her hand. Her headache grew worse as they stumbled along. She tripped over some vines. Whipping around, K.C. caught her as she fell forward. Her hair swung away from the left side of her head. K.C. gasped. Reaching out to her he gently touched her head.

"Ouch!" Jessie winced as pain shot through it.

"You've got a bad cut and bruise." His fingers came away with blood on them. "I didn't realize how badly you were hurt." His voice was full of concern. "Will you be okay for a bit?" he asked. "We can't stop yet."

"I'll be all right. Just don't walk so fast. I can't keep up." *How can I tell him that with each step my head throbs? It's the least of our problems.*

K.C.'s hand continued to grasp hers as they pushed through tangles of cat briar and wild blueberries. Groves of new growth white pine screened them as they fled. K.C. led them parallel to the back of the restaurant. They could hear loud voices now, yelling back and forth. Their pursuers were no longer trying to sneak up on them.

Soon they could see the back of the service station. K.C.'s car was parked outside.

"Jessie, when we break through the edge of the woods, run right to the car. Get in the back and lay on the floor. I think I left one of those old car blankets back there. Cover up, and don't move."

His free hand touched her lightly on the injured side of her head. She tried not to wince. There were no fresh bloodstains on his hand this time.

When they reached the paved area around the station, he released her hand. She ran across the pavement to the wall of the garage. Jessie inched her way to the edge of the building where K.C.'s car was parked. Crouching down, she made her way to the back door and slipped into the back seat. A green and brown plaid blanket lay on the floor. Lifting it she curled herself as small as possible on the floor and pulled the blanket over her. Dust tickled her nose. *Please don't let me sneeze,* she prayed. She waited, trembling as much from his lingering touch as from fear. Jessie had no choice but to trust him at this point. She was in no condition to continue to run on her own. Her body prickled with tension as she lay on the floor of the car for what seemed hours before she heard K.C.'s voice. "Thank you for the repair."

Jessie heard someone answer.

"If a couple of men come looking for me..." K.C.'s voice was louder now, "would you tell them you saw me heading south – alone?"

"Sure will, pal. Thanks for the twenty."

The car door opened, and she heard K.C. slip in. He started the engine and said in a low voice, "Stay down. I don't see them, but we aren't out of here yet."

The car moved slowly forward, gaining speed until she felt the rhythm of the road beneath her. K.C. made a sharp right, and the road became bumpy. All too soon, she felt the car shiver to a stop and wondered what was wrong.

"It's okay Jessie, you can sit up now."

She heard K.C. open his door. Pushing the blanket off she sat up. The door opened behind her. He reached in and lifted her from her hiding place grabbing the blanket as he swung her into his arms.

"I can walk," she protested.

"I'd rather carry you."

Her face grew hot with embarrassment. He had parked on a dirt road beside a meadow. They were well hidden away from the main road. Water gurgled nearby. Jessie felt the warmth of his arms beneath her. She looked everywhere but at him and saw a stream running through a cluster of trees, splashing over rocks in miniature waterfalls. Beside it there was an old apple tree, filled with fragrant blossoms, its gnarled roots sunk deep in the dirt at the stream's edge. K.C. gently set her down by the tree. She reached for the coarse trunk to keep her balance.

"We need to take care of that cut," he mumbled spreading the blanket at a mossy spot, then gesturing for her to sit. He strode briskly to the car returning in minutes with a small first aid kit.

Sitting on the blanket beside her, K.C. pulled her down until her head rested on his lap.

He opened the white plastic box filled with bandages and ointments. "Close your eyes," he instructed. Jessie obediently closed her eyes, but not before she caught his gaze and smiled her thanks.

K.C.'s hands moved gently as he wiped the dried blood away with a piece of medicated gauze. She winced slightly. Neither one of them said a word as he completed his caring for her wounds. Jessie felt peace for the first time in days. Finally he leaned back against the tree, her head still cradled on his lap. *What happened that made him afraid?* she wondered. *Should I risk his anger by asking?* She looked at his face. His eyes were closed. He looked so peaceful.

"K.C.? What frightened you as a child?"

His eyes flew open and he looked searchingly into hers. "Only my buddy from grade school knew," K.C. started, "but you and I have shared a nightmare that began a long time ago."

K.C.'s story began to unfold about a small boy who could have been anyone. *Perhaps*, she thought *this is the only way he can distance himself from his childhood nightmare.* All thoughts of being chased were forgotten as she listened attentively.

Chapter 16

Kimball Chase Avalon trudged along the stony trail that cut through the woods next to his school. With head bent in concentration, he viciously kicked stones out of his way and watched them fly up and bounce to the side of the path. His shoes stirred up the dry soil with each kick. The wind blew puffs of dirt into little swirling tornados around him. As often happened, that day he'd again been the focus of the local bully's malice. His third grade classmate, Roger Kincaid had been bullying Kim for some time and was making his life miserable. Roger's teasing voice echoed in his memory.

"Hey, Kimball the Pinball! How is the little girl, Kimmie?"

Kim received his worst teasing at school where others watched and laughed at his helplessness. He couldn't avoid Roger and his friends altogether and the uncertainty of when they'd meet terrified him.

Kim had never liked his name, the combination of his mother and grandmother's maiden names. He remembered when he was little, how proud his mother was as she told him Kimball meant "noble warrior," and Chase meant "Hunter." Little did he realize how prophetic his middle name would be. Even though his name would always remind him of his beloved mother, it still made him sound like a sissy.

"When I grow up, nobody is going to know my true name," he vowed that day.

He slowly drew his treasured New York Yankees baseball cap out of his pocket.

Smiling, he read Thurman Munson's name signed on the underside of the caps visor. He was only six when his dad took him to his first and only ball game. Getting Mr. Munson's autograph was the best thing that had ever happened to him. Two years ago his hero was the MVP of 1976. Kim wanted to be just like Mr. Munson. He was really special. Kim pulled the cap onto his curly brown hair and took the turn in the path that led through the deeper woods and to the back lot behind his house. Kim saw Elephant Rock ahead. The huge gray granite rock was Kim's favorite spot for pretending. It was here he conquered all the bullies in his life, and he was always the hero. Today it became the place of his undoing.

All pretending vanished as he was about to pass Elephant Rock. Roger and his buddies jumped out from behind it, shouting, "Here's Kimball the Pinball!" They stood arm in arm across the path, blocking Kim's way to safety at home. He tried running around them to the left. As one they shifted into his way.

"You can't get away from us," one of the boys taunted.

He tried to the right. Again they shifted as one. Their laughter added to his growing hate for them and anger at himself.

They surrounded him and everywhere Kim turned, one of them was there blocking his way. The wind blew across his sweat-covered body, chilling him. Suddenly they converged on him, wrestling his small body to the ground. One of the boys grabbed his baseball cap. Up in the air it flew, and another boy caught it. They threw his hat back and forth between them, laughing and taunting Kim.

"That's mine," cried Kim, "give it back." He scrambled to his feet and ran from one teasing classmate to the other. Suddenly, the cap was tossed high in the air where it twisted and turned as the wind buffeted it. The tangled branches of an oak tree above them stopped its descent.

"Like to see you get it now," yelled one of the heckling boys. They stood laughing and jeering at Kim's hopeless situation.

"Let's give him a lift," sneered another who went to the foot of the tree. Kim's thin, short frame was no match for the group that descended upon him. He kicked and fought as they each grabbed an arm or leg. Kim felt himself being lifted from the ground, then pushed higher, head first. He squirmed and twisted, but that made those holding him tighten their grip. He was given a final shove onto a high branch that caught him across his stomach. Suddenly he began to slip off. He desperately grasped the rough bark of the branch and swung one leg then the other onto the limb. Shaking, he pulled himself into a sitting position, his feet dangling below him. He sat trembling, weaving back and forth. Slowly he inched his bottom toward the tree's trunk. When he reached it, he wrapped his arms as far as they would go around. It felt so solid and safe.

Kim looked up. His hat dangled far above him. Hugging the trunk, he pulled his feet under him and reached for the next branch up. Carefully he maneuvered himself from branch to branch, staying near the tree's trunk until he was even with the one that held his beloved hat. While he climbed, the fall leaves obscured his vision. Now, looking far below, he realized he had gone way beyond an easy jump down. He watched as his tormentors tired of their game and walked away, scuffing through the dead leaves. They were laughing as they left him alone in the darkening woods.

Kim was miserable. He hadn't conquered the bullies. He was anything but a hero. He was tired, cold, and feeling very helpless.

The wind rustled through the leaves. *What do I do now? What would Thurman Munson do?* His spirits gradually lifted. "I think I can get it," he told himself. "I know I can!"

He reached up and grasped a branch above him. Steadying himself he stepped onto the limb on which his cap was caught.

Carefully letting himself down to a sitting position, he used his hands to inch his way out toward the cap. The branch began to tremble under his weight. He stopped for a moment and watched as his cap swung precariously from the end of the branch. Still sitting, he again scooted slowly across the rough textured branch toward his hat. Once again the branch trembled under his weight. Again Kim stopped. His hands hurt from gripping the coarse uneven bark.

The crackling of the leaves grew as the wind increased. One gust of wind shook the tree whipping around his cap and lifting it off the branch and into the air. It twisted and turned until it flew right in front of him. With no thought as to where he was, Kim reached out to grab his precious hat. With a long piercing scream, he fell forward from the limb. Whip-like branches struck his face and legs. He bounced from branch to branch until his fall was broken with a jerk. His jacket had snagged on a woody bough. He found himself dangling ten feet off the ground – afraid to move. His cap lay on the ground below.

Kim took a deep breath preparing to yell for help. Suddenly he felt his arms slipping out of his unbuttoned jacket. The branch swayed under his weight. He looked for other limbs, but there were none close enough to reach. Any movement would cause him to fall. He couldn't even yell. Slithering out of his jacket certainly wasn't an option, he had nowhere to go but down. Fear gripped him. Kim slowly crossed his arms in front of his chest to prevent sliding out of the jacket. Afraid to even breathe hard and risk falling, he allowed the tears that had been building behind his eyes to slip down his nose and drip off his chin. Shivering from cold and fright, Kim's misery was profound.

What seemed like hours later, a group of older boys were hiking through the woods when one of the boys found Kim's hat. As he bent to pick it up, he felt what he thought was a raindrop. Looking up another tear splashed on the young man's face and his gaze found Kim, hanging above them stiff and exhausted from his ordeal. Kim heard their excited voices below him but couldn't respond. Finally, one boy stood on another's shoulders and was able to reach him. Cautiously, the young man took the limp Kim in his arms and handed him down to his friends.

When Kim opened his eyes he realized he was home. The babysitter was bending over him, pulling the bedspread up to his chin.

***

"By sixth grade, things turned around for me," he told Jessie. "That was the year I began to grow taller and I filled out. In tenth grade I was nearly six feet tall, and no one ever called me names again."

"What happened to those bullies?"

"I made sure Roger and his buddies were no longer a threat." Jessie watched as K.C.'s forehead was transformed from a frown of remembered pain to jaw tightening purpose. "I made it into a game. With the help of another boy who was also the brunt of Roger's teasing. We hunted each of our tormentors. We made sure they paid for what they had done to us."

"What did you do? Did you hurt them?"

"Not physically."

"Your pain must have been great."

He nodded. "Quietly and subtly we took our revenge. They never knew it was my friend and I stalking them. Our retaliation was only partially satisfying. The incident in third grade left me with a paralyzing fear of heights. When I turned twenty-one, I never willingly told anyone my full name again."

Jessie let her hand fall to the top of his hand beside her, where it rested in sympathy.

"I understand the pain of teasing," she said. "Children can hurt each other for life."

Nothing more was said as K.C. and Jessie relaxed quietly, listening to the sounds around them. The water's burbling filled the silence and eventually, the soothing sound lulled Jessie to sleep.

K.C.'s finger traced the curve of Jessie's cheek as he watched her sleep. Her skin was so soft. The desire that had touched him earlier flowed through him in a way he'd not experienced before. It wasn't a longing to satisfy physical needs so much as a desire to protect and care for this fragile yet resilient person. *What is happening to me?* His finger continued across her cheek. He smoothed her hair, clearing it of tiny bits of grass and pebbles. His hand lingered above her wound daring not to touch it for fear he'd hurt her. Gently he cupped her cheek with his hand, caressing it slowly with his thumb until he also fell asleep.

Chapter 17

Jessie shivered. A cool breeze brushing across her arms woke her. She had been dreaming and didn't want to leave the comfort of it. She vaguely remembered something gently caressing her cheek and the pleasure it gave her. The strand of delight in the dream unraveled and slipped away. She opened her eyes. Her body was tucked in a fetal position, with her head on K.C.'s lap. The golden glow of the setting sun covered everything in a glorious warm blanket of color. Slowly, quietly she sat up. K.C. didn't move. His head was tilted against the bark of the tree. He was sound asleep. *He really must be exhausted.* She quietly made her way to some bushes, stretching her cramped body as she sought a private area to take care of other necessities. Afterward, Jessie wandered down to the stream, kneeling to splash cold water on her face to help wake up. Pushing back her hair, she touched the bandage and remembered K.C.'s tender care. The warm thought of his compassion turned chilly as she sensed someone watching her. Turning toward the apple tree, she found K.C. staring at her.

"I didn't want to wake you," she offered as she stood and moved towards him.

Turning, he picked up the blanket and nodded toward the car.

"Time to get going," he announced curtly.

Jessie was puzzled by his abruptness. Did she say or do something wrong? Did he think she was trying to run away again? Hurrying to the car, she slid into her seat.

"Are you going to try to drive straight through?" she asked. She glanced at him to gauge his mood. He sat unresponsive, a scowl on his face.

"No," he eventually answered. "I want to look for another motel for the night. We'll take a more roundabout way back to Everett tomorrow. I don't want to take the chance of running into any more trouble."

Jessie was amazed at the relief that flowed through her. She had one more day before facing the threat she'd left behind. A sudden thought surfaced, *one more day to be with K.C.* She shook her head, dismissing the brief rush of pleasure.

K.C. pulled onto the road, turned right at the next intersection, and soon pointed to a sign with "Jefferson, 8 miles." The sign included three terse words, "Food and Lodging." Neither of them said a word for the next four or five miles. Finally Jessie broke the silence.

"I knew it would be wonderful," she breathed.

K.C. glanced at her questioningly. Jessie gestured toward the sunset. The puzzled look that had creased his forehead smoothed out as he smiled in agreement. Neither spoke of their shared brush with death or the danger that might be following them.

They reached Jefferson just as it got dark. The blinking neon light of the "Bed and Bite" drew them. The parking lot was full of cars as they pulled into a space near the office door.

"Can I come in with you?" Jessie asked hesitantly.

"If you want."

She opened the door and slipped out to join him. She was hungry, tired, and badly needed a change of clothes. Everything was either dirty or bloody from their ordeal at the cliff. Maybe that was K.C.'s problem. Maybe she smelled. Pretending to scratch her head she took a few tentative sniffs under her arms. She didn't notice anything too terrible, a little sweat maybe.

"Hello there, what can I do for you?" The motel clerk's nametag read: Steve, Night Manager.

"We'd like a room with two beds please," K.C. replied as he reached for the sign-in pad. "Also, how late is the restaurant open?"

"You're in luck. Because of the Derby Wildflower Walks, we're keeping the restaurant open until 10:00 p.m." The man looked from Jessie to K.C. then back to her before lowering his gaze. *Why does he keep looking at me like that?* "We make good money on our rooms and food when that happens. Derby's the town next to us. Derby and Jefferson have some of the finest woodland wildflowers in the spring. There're even a couple of wild orchids, but only the experts know where, and they aren't telling. You might like to join in their walks..."

"Great!" Jessie broke into his enthusiastic monologue. She was starving.

Steve glanced again at her then quickly checked his computer.

He drew in a sharp breath, "Oh dear, I'm sorry folks."

Jessie sagged against the counter. *Not another glitch*?

"What is it?" K.C. asked.

"The last room we have only has one bed." Steve glanced from Jessie to K.C. "Will that do?"

"You've gotta be kidding?" K.C. groaned.

He must be remembering the uncomfortable arrangements at the last motel. Jessie nearly giggled until she remembered her aborted escape and K.C. sleeping on her bed.

"Please, any chance of getting a roll-away cot or something?" Jessie pleaded.

"I'm sorry, but we've rented out everything."

"Well, I guess it'll have to do," K.C. sighed. He pulled out his credit card and paid for the room.

"Room 230 on the backside, second floor."

"Can we eat first?" Jessie asked, "My stomach is growling."

K.C.'s eyes twinkled as he shook his head in mock disbelief. "So that's the grumble I've been hearing! We'd better change first. You look like you've been rolling in dirt and wildflowers!" He pulled a burr off Jessie's shirt.

Jessie felt her face warm as she blushed. The gnawing pain in Jessie's stomach would have to wait.

"Sure," Jessie replied, as she turned and headed for the car.

They drove around back to their room, grabbed their luggage, and headed up the outside stairway.

When K.C. opened the door, ushering her in, Jessie stopped short.

"Figures," she muttered.

Both had assumed the one bed would be king sized. It wasn't. It wasn't even a queen. It was a dinky double bed.

"And only one chair. Looks like I sleep on the floor tonight." K.C. shook his head resignedly.

After dumping her duffel, Jessie turned to him.

"Listen K.C., if you promise to stay on your side, we can share the bed."

"I promise!" K.C. said holding up a hand in a scouts honor sign.

Jessie stopped in front of the full-length mirror on the door. "I look terrible," she wailed. "Why did you let me go into the motel office? No wonder Steve kept looking funny at me. He must have thought you'd beaten me up." The gauze on her head was dirty and coming off, dried blood clung to her skin and dirt was all over her clothes, hair and skin. "I look like Pig-Pen from the Charlie Brown comics."

The reflection of K.C. grinning at her made her even more upset.

"You don't look so hot yourself," she smugly informed him stepping away from the mirror.

K.C.'s laughter changed to consternation. Turning, he rummaged in his bag until he found more bandages. Handing them to Jessie, he reached over to flick on the TV.

"Thanks." Pulling her Lee jeans and long sleeved pink and green Gap jersey from her duffle, Jessie headed for the bathroom. She closed the door with clear resolve. *No shower yet! A quick sponge bath will do me for now.* She replaced the bandage on her head and brushed her hair gently to clear it of snarls and twigs. Grabbing a pink elastic from her cosmetic bag, she pulled her hair back into a short ponytail. With a quick glance in the mirror she saw the perky teen of her high school days. *Nothing like a ponytail to keep one looking young.*

"I'm coming out now. Is it safe?"

"Sure."

K.C. had changed his jeans. This time he wore a gray and white cotton sweater. When she saw him, she couldn't help but appreciate how marvelous he looked. She noticed he was giving her the once over as well. *I wonder if he likes what he sees.*

"You could pass for my little sister!" he said with a laugh.

Little sister?

"Let's go." Clicking off the television, he grabbed her hand, pulling her along beside him. His touch sent a shiver of electricity up her arm. Suddenly her hand didn't feel like it belonged to her. She quickly looked away from him so he wouldn't see the shock on her face.

The rise and fall of conversations flowed around them as they entered the restaurant. The room was full. It looked like a family gathering in someone's kitchen. Apparently old and young alike found wildflowers fascinating. Checkered tablecloths with multicolored silk flowers graced each table and booth. Gingham curtains at the windows softened the log cabin look of the inside walls. Wagon wheel lights shone down on the tables and small lantern sidelights added to the warmth of the booths. Jessie felt happiness flood her at the thought of good food, a night's rest, and, for once, not being chased.

Smiling, she turned to K.C. and saw that he, too, was beaming. They both were caught up in the relaxed mood and festive atmosphere of the restaurant.

They slid into a booth away from the windows. It was tucked between a profusion of potted plants and another romantically lit booth.

It felt as if she had known K.C. for years rather than two days. Just being able to relax and do something normal changed the whole atmosphere between them. She studied the menu. Looking up, she came eye to eye with K.C. Swiftly he looked down at the menu in front of him. If she hadn't known better, she would have sworn the look in his eyes at that instant, was one of longing. *He must be as hungry as I am.*

"So, are you having the Family Pot Roast Dinner?" he asked, smiling as he referred to her huge breakfast and lunch.

"I sure feel like I could eat it all," she answered with a laugh, "but I can't eat a lot this late at night. Guess I'll just have the cheese and broccoli soup and a house salad. I want to save room for dessert."

K.C. chuckled, "Can't miss that dessert, huh! I have to admit they look good."

When the waitress arrived, K.C. told her what Jessie wanted.

"And bring me the Family Pot Roast Dinner," he added, turning to Jessie, "I'm going to try to tempt you a bit."

She couldn't be tempted. The dinner looked great, but she was looking forward to an ice cream puff with chocolate sauce and whipped cream! She always checked out the desserts before ordering.

K.C. finished off his pecan pie as she licked the last of the whipped cream and chocolate off her fork. Grinning, he leaned forward to wipe some of the cream from her nose with his napkin.

"K.C., from what you said, you were never going to tell anyone your real name. Why did you tell me?" His hand stopped midair.

Oh great, she thought, *I blew it again.* "Sorry, I'm being nosey. I didn't mean to bring up bad memories."

"It's okay," he said as he finished wiping the cream from the tip of her nose, "Even though I was bullied and abused as a kid, I've been able to let it go. Now, I can actually laugh about all the times I was assigned to the girls locker rooms or had something addressed to Miss Kim Avalon."

"You still haven't told me why you shared your real name with me." she persisted.

"I don't know," he said with a puzzled look. Then he looked straight at her, a smile playing around the corners of his mouth. "You have a way about you, Miss Jessie. Thank you for not laughing when I told you."

"I've had some pretty unusual nicknames myself," she offered, "Jessie James and Jessie "Under-a-ton" were a couple. I know how names can hurt."

"Now that I've shared one of my deepest secrets with you, don't you think it's time to share one with me?"

"Oh, I don't have any deep dark secrets."

"How about why you looked so sad and started to cry when I asked about your family? Especially when you talked about your sister Jen. There was something more than just being lonely, wasn't there?"

This time it was her turn to look away in pain.

"Sorry Jessie. Now I'm being nosey." He laid his hand lightly over hers.

She felt its warmth and looked up.

"No, it's only fair," she said, leaving her hand beneath his.

"When I went to college in the mid-west, I met this terrific guy. His name was Jeff Simmons. We dated a bit our freshman year and then got more serious during our sophomore year." She gazed past K.C. as she remembered the man she had thought of as her prince charming.

"He had a blond crew cut and the bluest eyes I'd ever seen. He was funny, too. He was always bringing me fun gifts. Late at night he'd throw rocks at my dorm window, and I'd let down a rope. He'd tie a basket to it with goodies in it or even some poetry he'd written. He was always surprising me with something special. He had a big family who always expected him for the holidays, so I was never able to bring him home. I did go to his family's house for a couple of holidays, but I missed being with my own family."

"Sounds like both of you were really happy." K.C. said.

"Oh yes, we were. We talked about getting engaged that year, and eventually getting married. Jen was a junior in High School by then and was looking at colleges she wanted to attend. I invited her to stay with me and take a look around my college. She came and met Jeff for the first time. It wasn't as if I hadn't talked about him. I even had pictures of Jeff and me to show my family. But…you…see, Jennifer is quite lovely. She always was beautiful, even as a baby. Her hair is very blond, not a dirty blond like mine. Her eyes are a deep blue, and they actually sparkle when she is excited."

"Don't tell me," K.C. said, his smile gone. "Jeff fell for your sister."

"Hook, line and sinker, the stinker." she replied, "He transferred to a college near the one Jen eventually chose and they eloped at the end of her freshman year. They've been in California since then. I thought I would die of a broken heart."

"You must have been devastated. How did you end up in New York?"

"I wanted to get as far away as possible so I chose a grad school in New England. I haven't seen my sister since she got married."

K.C. held both of her hands in his. Jessie looked down at his large hands enveloping her smaller ones. They sat for a few seconds in silence. He gently released his hold on her.

"Let's head back to the room," he said, pushing his chair back. "It's getting late, and we should leave early to get to Everett. I don't want to run into those guys again."

Their quiet interlude was over and reality crashed back into their thoughts. They walked back to the room in silence. K.C.'s hand brushed hers as he reached for the motel key. His touch left her breathless.

Chapter 18

Jessie, showered and ready for bed, peeked out the bathroom door looking for K.C. He was looking out the window, his back to her. *Checking for men in black?* Taking advantage of his distraction, she dashed for the bed, pulling the covers up to her chin. Hugging her side of the bed, she faced the wall.

"Bathroom's free," she called.

She heard the window drapes rustle and turned in time to see K.C. push the drapes apart and let in a gleam of faint moonlight. Her covers now came to the bridge of her nose. He glanced at her on his way to the bathroom. She thought he stifled a cough, but when the door closed he exploded into laughter. *I am not funny*, she fumed and faced the wall once again.

She was nearly asleep when she heard him whisper.

"Jessie?" K.C. softly called as he shut off the bathroom light. She didn't make a sound.

K.C. lifted the top blanket. She rolled closer to her edge of the bed and gripped the mattress holding herself there.

"Jessie, I'm going to sleep on top of the bedspread. You can relax. I won't even be able to touch you by accident."

She tried to relax as he thumped his pillow a few times before he lay down. A double bed certainly didn't leave much room for moving around. She hadn't realized how close he would be even if they weren't skin to skin.

She turned over and unexpectedly began to roll toward the middle of the bed. *Whoa! Will I have to hold onto the mattress all night?* His body filled most of the bed weighing it down so she'd sink toward the middle. She rolled back to the edge of the mattress again digging her fingers into the sheet to keep from slipping.

Jessie searched for other things to think about. *What would they do when they reached his apartment? Did he mean what he said? Would he check out her story? If he reneged, would he stop me from leaving?* Slipping into a deep sleep she dreamed again of running and getting nowhere. The sounds of someone behind her were getting closer. She was frantic and screamed when suddenly there was a man in front of her. It was K.C. She was safe now and ran into his arms. He pushed her behind him where she clung to him.

Pale light brightened the room as Jessie surfaced from her dream. She was lying against K.C.'s back, her arms wrapped around him, her head tucked into his neck. The spicy smell of his skin and the softness of his hair against her forehead were comforting. She didn't move, but lay savoring this moment of contentment. She felt safe. Too soon, K.C. began to stretch and wake. Jessie quickly pulled away, rolling out of bed. It was almost 6 am. She headed for the bathroom before he could see how much his closeness had affected her.

What a dream! She looked into the mirror. *At least I look rested.* She changed into her flowered print T-shirt and jeans and went back into the bedroom to start packing her duffel.

"Jessie, we have to talk."

Did he know I had my arms around him last night? She was afraid to turn around.

"Jessie? Are you ok?"

Jessie slowly faced him. "Sorry, just concentrating on my packing."

"I have a friend on the police force in Everett. His name is Detective Derek Alexander. I think we should meet with him."

"I don't trust the police in Everett."

"You can trust him." K.C. moved toward her as he continued. "He's a good friend and I've also worked with him."

"I don't know. I'll have to think about it." She picked up her duffel and started for the door. "I'm hungry. Let's have breakfast." The sooner they were with other people, the safer she would feel with her own emotions.

They stowed their luggage in the car and went to eat. The cozy restaurant of the previous night was now filled with a bright glare of sunlight streaming through windows that fronted the building. Brilliant light even reached the deepest corners of the room. There was nowhere to hide if they'd needed to. The booths were full so the waitress led them to a table in the middle of the room. Jessie looked nervously around. So far there were no men in black. She relaxed.

"The specials today are Eggs Benedict and Pecan Waffles."

"They both sound good," Jessie sighed. At last there was something safe to focus on – food.

"I've got a great idea." K.C. grinned at her. "Lets get one of each and split. That way you can enjoy both."

"I like the way you think, Mr. Avalon," she said with a smile.

K.C. was turning out to be an interesting and complex man.

"Tell me about Derek," she asked as they ate.

"Derek is an old friend," K.C. replied. "In fact he was the new kid I told you about back in the third grade."

"How did you get connected with him?"

"Derek was a loner like me because of Roger and his friends. One day Derek ran to Elephant Rock in tears. I was already there in much the same state."

"It makes me so mad." Jessie thumped the table with her fist. "To think a bunch of bullies have that kind of power."

"A defender of the underling, I see," he chuckled.

"I've seen it at my school, too. It's so unfair. Is that when you became friends?"

"Yep! As soon as we got over our embarrassment, we made a pact to make Roger and his friends pay for our humiliation. That's when we started to pal around. He helped me with my 'game.'"

"What exactly did you two do to Roger and friends?"

"For two years we followed them, sabotaging their plans, stealing the notes they'd hide to each other. We wreaked havoc on them and they never knew who was doing it."

"You sure were vindictive."

"It was one way to help recoup our self esteem. But it paid off in other ways, too."

"How was that?"

"We both went off to college. Derek went on to the police academy. He told me once that our 'game' helped him in his police training. He is quite a master of disguises, for one. He can tail someone so unobtrusively that he can be steps behind them without their knowing."

"So you stayed friends?"

"Oh yah, we've always stayed in touch. When he came back to Everett, he'd help me occasionally with my work, and I've helped him. Now is a time when we can use his expertise."

"I think I'll like Derek," she answered, "and I need all the help I can get."

"Then we'd better start if we want to get to Everett by lunch time."

K.C. paid the check, and they were on the road. Jessie looked behind them for suspicious black cars. So far there was none.

"Jessie, help navigate these back roads for me. There's a New York map in the glove compartment." K.C. pointed to a door near her knees.

"Don't you have a GPS?"

"Yep! It's in the glove compartment."

"Why don't you use it?"

"It will send me on interstates. I want some of the smaller roads."

Opening the glove compartment, she saw the GPS lying on top of a couple of maps. She carefully slid them out from under it.

"Oh!" The maps fell to her lap.

"What's wrong?"

"Is…is that a real gun in there?" she stammered, pointing to a gun tucked in the bottom of the glove compartment.

"Well, yah. That's my .38 special revolver. Sometimes I need it on tougher jobs," he admitted.

"Have you ever shot anyone?"

"No, and I don't want to, either. It can be a good convincer just by its presence, but there's always the possibility I might have to use it."

Jessie gingerly shut the door on the glove compartment and found the NY map. They rode in companionable silence as they made their way through back roads, drawing closer and closer to the town she so recently had run from in panic.

At about 1:30 pm they slipped into Everett from a side road and pulled into the parking lot of a large brick building.

"You live in one of these apartments?"

"Yep, that corner one on the left," he pointed, pulling around back to his parking space.

K.C. grabbed their luggage as Jessie unwound herself from the map and her seat belt.

They approached the front door where he handed her his key while propping himself against the open screen door. "You can order a pizza for lunch. I'll call Derek."

"Sounds good to me."

"I hope one pizza will be enough," K.C. teased her.

"One is fine," she answered, "as long as it has eggplant and peppers on it."

Shaking his head, K.C. led the way. The living area opened up to a small dining room, and off that was the kitchen. One wall of the living room was lined, floor to ceiling, with books. In front of the bookcase was a black leather recliner, a free standing reading light, and to its right, a table. A couch was the only other large piece of furniture.

"I didn't know you liked to read. I would have thought you were more an action kind of person."

She stepped to the bookcase and read the spines of some of the books: *Great Cases of Scotland Yard, The Complete Sherlock Holmes,* and *Unsolved Crimes of the Twentieth Century.*

"You lean toward detective stories, I see."

"I find them fascinating. I try to figure out some of the unsolved ones," he replied as he joined her. "Some are quite a challenge. Do you enjoy reading?"

"I love it. My favorites are romances and biographies. Romances for what might be and biography for what really was."

"The pizza number is posted on the fridge," K.C. directed. "They deliver here all the time. Give them a call, and order what you like. When you're done, I'll call Derek."

Jessie ordered the pizza, then pulled out one of K.C.'s books and leafed through it as he made his call to Derek.

"Hi Derek – K.C. I need your help." Jessie couldn't help overhearing the conversation as she sat flipping through the book.

"It's a sensitive problem – you might say a matter of life and death. Can you come by – about 5:30? Stay for supper. Great…Bye."

Twenty minutes later they were finishing off a very stringy pizza with eggplant, peppers, onions and mushrooms.

"K.C., I really need some things from my apartment."

"Not a good idea, Jessie. I'd rather keep an eye on you here."

"Still don't trust me!" she fumed.

"It's not that! It's possible that your apartment is being watched. You could be in danger going back."

"What am I going to do? I've been wearing the same clothes for a week. Could you go?"

"I'm afraid they know me, too," K.C. retorted. "At the restaurant when you took off? They walked right by me – looked right at me. They knew who I was. I saw them at Mrs. Spaulding's house when I met with her."

"I told you they're Mrs. Spaulding's men. They're the ones who did the killing."

"Didn't you say you slipped out of a back door from your apartment building? I'm pretty good at dodging and hiding myself. I could slip back in that way and retrieve what you need."

"I could go too," she ventured.

"No!" She recoiled as his words struck her like an invisible hand.

"No," he said again, this time softening his command as he took her hands. "I don't want anything to happen to you. You're much safer here. Just don't leave the apartment!"

She knew he was right. It was strange, but she did feel safer with him. There were no more handcuffs, and, if she had to, she could leave the apartment when he was gone. She still wasn't sure if she should trust him completely. Was he still thinking of taking her to Mrs. Spaulding? Was he afraid of losing his commission? Jessie put aside those thoughts and asked for a pencil and paper. She jotted down a list of things she wanted and where to find them.

Jessie looked up from her list when K. C. came out of his bedroom wearing the filthiest, torn clothes she'd ever seen.

"Oh, no!" she gasped.

K.C. jumped with surprise. "Do I look that bad?"

"Sorry, I just remembered my plants. I went off in such a panic, I forgot about my plants."

"You're worried about plants? How many do you have?"

"Just a few." She looked at him hopefully. "Could you water them while you're there?"

"If they haven't died already," he grumbled, turning abruptly and leaving.

She was sure he was annoyed with her. *Why did I ask about my flowers?* He didn't need extra errands. Jessie went to the kitchen window that faced the parking lot and watched K.C. drive away.

At last she was alone and unexpectedly Jessie didn't feel so safe anymore.

Chapter 19

K.C. smiled as he fingered the holes at the knees of his grimy jeans. He tugged at them until he heard the rip of fabric. *Better.* He noticed the bottom edges of the pant legs were raveling out nicely as well. His worn flannel shirt felt soft against his chest. He'd hated the thought of throwing out his favorite work shirt. Now the shirt joined his disguise collection. Slipping on his dark glasses, a floppy cowboy hat, and ratty brown leather vest, he felt he was ready. *Can't hide my 6-foot height,* he thought. *If I bend over like someone with a stomachache, maybe I'll look like a homeless person with back problems.*

Just in case he ran into trouble, he slipped the .38 out of the glove compartment and tucked it into the waistband of his pants where it was hidden behind the vest. K.C. locked the car, then shuffled slowly toward Jessie's apartment three buildings away. His eyes darted back and forth observing all around him.

People passed him, going out of their way to not get too near. *What a bonus*, he thought as he noticed trashcans set out for collection. He stopped occasionally and pretended to rummage in them. Lifting a bag, he held it near his face and nearly gagged. Holding it away, he pretended he was looking at it while he turned, scanning the cars parked up and down the street. He didn't pause when one car in particular caught his attention. Shoving the bag's foul contents back into the garbage, he surreptitiously looked again. A black Mercedes! It was parked at the front of Jessie's building. He could just make out two figures slouched in the front seat. Ducking into the doorway of a building near him and then another, he was able to slip into an alley that ran along the back of her apartment complex.

K.C. easily picked the outside lock and cautiously slipped up the back stairs to her floor then down the hall to her apartment. Using her keys, he quietly let himself in. He carefully peeked out the front window. The Mercedes was just as he'd seen it. Everything was quiet. No one suspected he was there.

K.C. took a deep breath and straightened from his bowed position with some pain. He finally saw what home was like for Jessie.

Straight ahead of him, a vintage poster of "The Perils of Pauline" hung on the wall above her desk. "Figures," he mumbled.

Next to her desk, filling the wall, were bookcases.

"She wasn't kidding when she said she liked to read." He shook his head in disbelief.

Even though the apartment was small, it was neatly arranged. It was also alive with her "few plants". Every room within view was a jungle of hanging, sitting, blooming plants. When he went to her bedroom, he found plants lining the windowsill. He couldn't resist a peek into the bathroom and, hanging near the shower, was a green striped spidery looking plant. With a sigh, he checked her list and started his search. Her neatness made finding clean clothes and cosmetics easy, especially since he wasn't really sure about the names of some of the things she'd written down. He opened several dresser drawers until he found what she wanted and pulled out the requested clothes. Selecting the underwear gave him pause. Riffling through a woman's dresser was sometimes part of his job, because he was usually looking for something contraband. However, he'd never been in a woman's dresser drawers to choose her clothing. Gingerly, he plucked out what looked good to him and tossed them on the bed with the other things he had gathered. He needed a large black trash bag, and he found a box of them in the kitchen cupboard. Carefully, he placed the clothing and other accessories into it. He would draw less attention as a street person if he had a trash bag in tow.

K.C. quietly left the apartment. He set the bag of clothing at the head of the back stairs and then slipped down the front steps to the mailboxes in the entryway. The key to Jessie's mailbox was on the same chain as her apartment key. *There might be something here she wants.* K.C. turned the key and the door of the box slammed into the wall as letters, advertisement and papers tumbled onto the floor. He gathered the armful of mail from the floor and quickly looked out the glazed glass in the front door. Did the noise alert the men out front? Even though he couldn't see details outside, someone might be able to see movement on the inside. Nothing seemed to be happening.

Suddenly he remembered the plants. He'd forgotten to water them. Running up the stairs he made a dash for the trash bag, dumping the mail inside. If he hurried, he might be able to do a quick watering. Fumbling with the key, he remembered seeing a watering can on the floor near the kitchen sink. K.C. began a frenzied dance from sink to plants, sink to plants.

With the last plant watered, he looked out the window at the car below and into the face of one of the men who stood there. Throwing the can into the sink, he dashed out the door, grabbed the bag, and clattered down the back steps. The sound of smashing glass and splintering wood at the other end of the apartment complex propelled him out the rear entrance. He ran down the alley, not stopping until two of the buildings were behind him.

Hunched over again, he leisurely picked at trash in a garbage can. Surreptitiously looking towards Jessie's place, he saw the

Mercedes still there, the car doors ajar. Two men in black were running out of the building, looking up and down the street as they did. *They'll have a harder time recognizing me in the twilight. I should be safe*

Turning away, trash bag bumping behind him, K.C. trudged along the street toward the lot where his car was parked. He stopped to pick up some trash and then discard it. He didn't dare look back. His progress was slow, but his heart was racing. He had nearly been caught. Would they wonder about the homeless man who now carried a bulging trash bag?

Chapter 20

Jessie slid onto K.C.'s leather recliner. Leaning back into the chair, she turned her head and inhaled deeply. It still smelled like new leather. She stroked the smooth surface of the arms. They were slightly warm to the touch as if K.C. had just been leaning on them. She felt enveloped by the chair's top and sides as they cradled her smaller body. She reached for the Sherlock Holmes book she'd left on the nearby table and flipped through the pages. Soon she was engrossed in one of the stories.

Straining to see the words, she unconsciously reached for the light above her, switching it on. She finished the story and returned the book to the table, suddenly aware that the pool of yellow light surrounding her was the only light in a now shadowy apartment.

What happened to the time? She looked out a window and saw the streetlights glowing and the sky dark. *Where was K.C.? Did something happen to him?*

She hadn't realized how late it had become.

Don't get nervous, Jessie. Tension tightened her shoulders. *Keep occupied.*

"I know – I'll make some supper." Jessie spoke aloud to break the silence. She went around turning on lights before she went to the refrigerator.

"What a mess," she groaned as she surveyed the shelves of dried up veggies and curdled milk. He obviously hasn't been home for a while. With a jolt she remembered why.

He'll be angry if you mess with his food, she told herself. *Someone has to take care of him...it.* Flustered, she opened the trash and threw out the worst.

All that remained were a few decent carrots, two onions, and two slightly wrinkled peppers and some condiments. A single frozen steak and some frost-covered mystery items in plastic bags graced the small freezer. The upper cupboards of the kitchen held little except salt, sugar, and maple syrup. *You'd think all that sweet stuff would have helped his disposition.*

She stopped by the kitchen window and looked down into the parking lot. The lights illuminated some of the area but left others hidden in gloom. She could just make out K.C.'s space. It was still empty. *Where is he?*

Turning, Jessie fumbled through the bottom cupboards and found frying pans and spoons and soon had a stir-fry going on the stove. One of the mystery bags contained spinach, which she added to the stir-fry. K.C. was full of surprises. She wondered if he believed the Popeye jingle and felt he got his strength from spinach. Jessie imagined him standing in a Popeye pose, his muscles popping out like basketballs. Her laughter echoed in the empty apartment.

The sound of someone in the hall brought an unexpected surge of joy. She ran to the door, but the click of another door opening and closing dashed her expectations.

She dragged herself back to the kitchen and put her stir-fry on simmer. *Now what? Oh, yes, dessert.* How could she be creative there? She remembered seeing an open bag of chocolate chip cookies. With what was left of some vanilla ice cream in one of the mystery packages, she made three large ice cream sandwiches. Wrapping them in waxed paper, she put them back into the freezer to firm up. Jessie set the table to keep from thinking about K.C. and what might have happened to him. The silverware in her hands shook.

Jessie again looked out the window at the parking lot. K.C.'s spot was still empty but a black car had pulled next to his parking place. A man in black stepped out of the car, looked around, then looked up at her window. She jumped back out of sight. *They found me.*

K.C., she silently cried, *I need you.*

Footsteps again sounded on the stairs. *How did they find me?*

Jessie stood in the living room watching the doorknob turning back and forth. She'd locked the door when K.C. left. Now she saw the chain above the door. She quickly slipped it into place.

Another set of footsteps. *That's right. There were two of them.*

Jessie ran to the kitchen, fumbled in the knife drawer and pulled out a huge butcher knife. The metal gleamed, the point looked very sharp. *Ugh! Too messy.* Instead she tossed it back into the drawer and turned to the cupboard, grabbing a large frying pan. Jessie pulled one of the chairs from the table and stood on it behind the door. The frying pan wobbled as she held it high over her head.

A key rattled in the lock. *They have a skeleton key.* She felt a scream rising in her throat.

The door opened and was held fast by the chain.

"What's wrong?" The deep voice of one of the men questioned.

"I don't know."

Was that K.C.'s voice? He's here! Instead of a scream, a squeak escaped.

"Jessie? Are you all right? Why's the chain on?"

Jessie jumped down from the chair, slid the frying pan under the recliner and thrust the chair back under the table.

She pushed the door closed and loosened the chain. The door opened. "I'm so glad your back, they've found us."

"What do you mean?"

"A black car is parked out back next to your spot, and a man in black got out and saw me in the window."

Jessie pulled on K.C.'s arm. He dropped the black trash bag and hurried to the kitchen where he deposited a bag of Chinese take-out onto the counter.

"Show me."

"There." Jessie cautiously approached the window and pointed to where the black car sat.

K.C. burst into laughter.

"Why are you laughing?"

"Turn around and look back at the front door."

Standing there was a tall man dressed in a black turtleneck, pants and black sports jacket. His wavy black hair gleamed in the light of the apartment. Jessie gasped. He seemed to feel right at home as he slipped off his coat and put it on the back of one of the chairs at the table.

"Jessie, this is Derek."

"Well, hello!" a deep voice rumbled as Derek walked toward Jessie. "Are you the sensitive situation K.C. needs to talk to me about? You look more like life than death to me."

Jessie felt foolish.

K.C. noticed the set table and he sniffed the air.

"What is that delicious smell?"

"Supper," she meekly replied going to the stove to check on the stir-fry. "I see you've been busy, too." She waved a free hand at the Chinese food. He was grinning, his dimples deepening. *He doesn't smile as much as he should.*

"I guess I'd better put my meager Chinese offering away." K.C. opened the refrigerator and put his package inside. Touching her shoulder, he pointed to the black heap sitting on the living room floor. "Your clothes are in the trash bag."

Jessie looked at him in disbelief. "Did you clean out my whole apartment?"

"No! But I nearly got caught. They were out front watching." Jessie was very aware of Derek watching her as she sauntered to the bag, struggled as she hefted it onto the couch, and started pulling things out.

"What in the world is this stuff?" she asked as papers and letters tumbled out. "You sure were thorough."

Her mail lay scattered on top of the couch. She sat down next to it and began to sort.

K.C. went to change.

"Are you a friend of K.C.'s?" Derek asked sitting in the recliner across from her.

The question really threw her. What was she to K.C.? A job? A case? A friend? Or could she be something more? She was saved from answering as K.C. came back into the room.

Jessie noticed appreciatively that his vagabond disguise gone and he had donned jeans and a maroon sweater.

"Thanks for coming, Derek. We'll talk after we eat. This is Jessie Overton."

"I've been watching her unveil the contents of her garbage."

Jessie shot Derek a dark look. *Who does he think he is? K.C.'s friend, that's who,* she admonished herself.

"I believe Jessie has produced a miracle supper from my meager supplies. Shall we eat?"

Jessie caught Derek watching at her. *What's his problem?* She left her sorting and went to the kitchen. *Can I really trust K.C.'s friend?* She was beginning to wonder. *If not, I'm going to need a bigger miracle than this stir-fry.*

Chapter 21

Jessie silently studied the intriguing man who sat opposite her at the dinner table. She noticed Derek's quick decisive gestures as he and K.C. talked. The police detective's eyes were constantly moving…observing. *Pay attention to K.C.,* she wanted to tell him after she caught his eyes lingering on her for what must be the tenth time.

"Jessie?" K.C. turned and caught her watching Derek. K.C. frowned at her. A flicker of anger lit his eyes, then was gone. Maybe she imagined it.

"Do you want to tell Derek your story?"

"You do it, I've relived it so many times I don't think I can get through it again."

K.C.'s account was a brief and concise narrative that could have happened to someone else.

"So you see, my friend, if what Jessie told me is true – after we were chased by those thugs, I tend to believe her – she could be in terrible danger."

Jessie was amazed at what she'd just heard. He actually says he believes her. The relief and elation she felt was incredible.

"Well, I believe her," Derek replied looking right at her. His eyes steady for the first time. "And not just because Jess is beautiful and a great cook."

She could feel the blood rush to her face. *What an irritating man.* K.C. was watching her with that frown again.

"How is it you believe her story so quickly?" K.C. demanded angrily, turning back to Derek.

"I have an advantage over you, pal," Derek remarked, soothing K.C.'s anger. "We've been following Mrs. Spaulding's activities for quite some time. Her husband was a local gangster. We have some evidence of gambling and money laundering."

"Derek...buddy. I could have helped you out! All this right in my own backyard, and I never realized it. In fact it was Mrs. Spaulding who hired me to find Jessie."

"We've been trying to keep our investigations low key, K.C. If I'd known you'd been called in by them, I would have clued you in."

"What about Mrs. Spaulding's husband? When she called me in with this job, there wasn't any sign of her husband."

"We're not sure. He disappeared a couple of years ago, and she claims he's on an extended business trip. We believe his wife is carrying on his work. The one thing we lacked was eyewitness evidence to make the first move. Several times we were close. The evidence was within our grasp and then the person of interest would disappear or have an unfortunate accident. We think someone inside the department is selling us out."

"What? Are you now saying I could become evidence that disappears!" Jessie interjected. She was beginning to get angry. *If they had put a stop to Mr. and Mrs. Spaulding long ago, I wouldn't have had to go through this last horrendous week.*

"You have to do something!" Exasperated, she pounded her fist on the table making the dishes rattle.

"She sure is feisty, isn't she?" Derek leaned lazily back in his chair, his tense movements gone. *He's laughing at me.* Jessie looked from Derek to K.C.

"She constantly amazes me," K.C. said, shaking his head in agreement. Both were watching her. "One moment she's meek and the next she's fighting and spitting."

Suddenly serious, Derek sat up, looked into her eyes, and took hold of her hands. She felt like a mouse, spellbound, having come face to face with a large black cat. She trembled.

"Jess, the only way we can do something is with your help. We need you to identify the police officer you saw at the house. With him out of the way and you as our witness, we can nail the whole gang. Are you willing to do this?"

The trembling at his touch changed to a shiver of fear, but he held her hands steady and waited for her answer. *I want an end to this. I want to be free of the fear.* Jessie knew her only choice was to stop running and identify those who were responsible.

"Ye-e-es…yes, I'm willing."

"Don't worry," Derek continued. "After you identify the man, we'll put you in a safe house until the trial. No one will know where you are except a few trusted officers on the force."

"Will K.C. know?" she asked, looking at K.C. for the first time.

"If you want him to," Derek answered, letting go of her hands and turning to K.C.

K.C. was sitting with his fists clenched, glaring at them, waiting for her answer.

"Oh, yes, please! I want K.C. to know. Can he be there, too?"

She watched K.C.'s fists unclench and an idiotic smile slowly spread across his face. K.C. looked at Derek expectantly.

"I'm afraid not, Jess. It would only complicate things. I have four good men who will be there, so you don't need to worry."

Her feeling of disappointment surprised her. K.C. didn't look happy either.

"What do we do now?" K.C. asked, reaching across the dinner table for her hands. His warm fingers covered her cold ones and gave them a squeeze.

Jessie at last felt vindicated. Derek had assured her that she wasn't imagining all that she had recently experienced, and K.C. now knew the truth of the situation as well. Safety was in sight.

"Tomorrow I'm going to bring over some of the tools of my trade. I don't know if K.C. has told you, but we used to pal around together when we were kids."

"He did mention something of the sort," she replied with a grin. "He said you are a master of disguise."

"Thanks. At last you admit it!" Derek gave K.C. a gentle punch on the shoulder. Turning back to Jessie, he continued.

"I'm going to bring over some supplies, and we'll make you into someone even your family won't recognize. Then we'll go to the department and see if you can identify our mole."

"Will I go as a journalist? Or suspect?"

"To get you by security, we're going to have to say you're an undercover cop in disguise and on assignment from another town. OK with you?"

"Sure. I'd rather be a cop than a suspect." Jessie glanced at a wall clock as she stifled a yawn. *Is it nine o'clock already?*

"Are you staying here?" asked Derek.

Suddenly she realized her predicament. This wasn't a motel room. This was a man's apartment. She couldn't go to her apartment.

"Well…um…I guess so. I really don't know where else I'd go. At least I feel safe here with K.C."

"You could always stay at my apartment," Derek suggested with a mischievous grin. "I'll make you breakfast, and I even have a guest room I think you'd like."

Jessie frowned as she looked to K.C. for direction.

"Thanks for the offer, pal," K.C. said, standing with an outstretched hand to say goodbye. "But I think Jessie and I can make things work out here for the night. We've managed so far."

As K.C. walked Derek to the door, Jessie cleared the table and started running hot water for the dishes.

"Good-bye, Jess. See you tomorrow." Derek called from the living room. "If you have any trouble with my friend here, give me a call. My offer stands."

Her hands were deep in suds when she felt K.C. standing behind her, his hands gently touching her shoulders. His voice was whispery soft near her ear as he bent to speak.

"Do you mind terribly staying here?"

Jessie leaned lightly against his chest.

"I really feel safest right here where you are," she answered. She could feel the rapid beating of his heart against her and longed to turn and have him hold her in his arms. Her soapy hands lingered just out of the water. Then the moment passed as he moved to her side, grabbing a dishtowel.

"K.C., thank you for believing in me and my story."

"I was sure you were spinning me a wild tale until those men showed up."

"You said when you grabbed me that you really needed the money. If I'm not being too nosey again, are you in real financial trouble?"

"Let's just say my work isn't very steady, and I'm on the low end of the financial ladder right now."

"Have you thought of doing anything else?"

"I've tried different things but was never able to stick with them for long. It's funny, but I've been thinking about that just today, that I needed to find something more steady."

Jessie's heart skipped a beat. What would make him consider a full time job at a time like this?

"Tell me what happened when you went to my apartment. We haven't had a chance to talk about it yet."

They worked together as K.C. described his adventure at her apartment and his appreciation for her tastes in décor and reading. They began talking about the romances she read.

"I love happy endings," she said as the water drained from the sink. "Even though, in reality, not every life ends happily, people still experience special moments that live in their memories forever."

"You are a romantic!" K.C. chuckled. Turning away from her, he suddenly became serious. "What you've been going through hasn't been pleasant."

"Oh, I don't know about that," she said with a grin as she followed him into the living room. She grabbed the trash bag of clothes from the couch and headed for K.C.'s bedroom.

"By the way, where are you going to sleep?" she called out from his bedroom.

The sudden sound of squeaks and thuds startled her, and she ran back to the open bedroom door. Her mail had been tossed on the table and the couch had been transformed into a double bed.

"Can I at least have some sheets, pillow, and blanket?" he inquired with a grin.

She playfully blocked his way stepping backward as he advanced into the room. K.C. strode to the closet, opened the door, and rummaged around on a shelf. She stood behind him gaping. Along with the usual male wardrobe, hanging in the corner of the closet were several women's dresses with large women's shoes beneath them. His arms full of linens, he closed the closet door with a slam and headed for the living room. Jessie ran to the bedroom door and stood in his way. She had a few questions to ask. K.C. tossed the linens over her head onto the living room floor. Then, placing his hands around her waist, he picked Jessie up and moved her out of his way. Before releasing her, he planted a kiss on her forehead. K.C. turned to the couch and enthusiastically started to make his bed. Jessie stood astonished for a minute, turned, and gently closed the door behind her.

Chapter 22

K.C. heard the click of the door closing behind him. Stopping his frantic bed making, he sank heavily on the bed, holding his head in his hands. It had taken all of his strength not to kiss her and crush her in his arms.

His thoughts turned to Derek. His friend seemed to have captivated Jessie. K.C. had noticed how she couldn't keep her eyes off him. He was glad they'd confided in Derek, but, in light of the detective's knowledge of the Spaulding affair, K.C. felt like a fool.

K.C. punched his pillow – hard. *Why did I treat her so badly? Will she ever trust me?* He laid down and pulled up the blanket – but sleep refused to come. Questions whirled through his mind as he tossed and turned. Over the years, he had pushed himself to be physically strong. But where had it gotten him? How could he expect her to care for him in any way except for protection? Would Jessie ever see him as more than a bodyguard?

The closeness of her presence was becoming dangerously tempting. The sooner she was in the safe house, the safer she would be – especially from him.

Chapter 23

Ding-dong…ding-dong…ding-dong. "All right…all right I'm coming."

Jessie stepped into the living room in time to see K.C. jump out of bed and unlock the door. Derek had arrived at eight a.m. sharp with an armload of grocery bags, boxes, and some sort of case slung over his shoulder.

Jessie laughed. He looked like a peddler.

"I have donuts, milk, bread, and three coffees," he announced following her into the kitchen. "I wasn't sure if you had anything for breakfast." He dropped the grocery bags on the counter.

Jessie rummaged through the cupboards and refrigerator looking for other breakfast supplies. She discovered a carton with three eggs tucked way in the back.

"Hey, beautiful! Do you like coffee?" Derek turned back to the living room without waiting for an answer and deposited the boxes and case on the floor.

K.C. had put the couch back together and she noticed her mail was once again scattered across the cushions.

"Sorry, afraid not," she called to him. "I'm a hot chocolate person, but I know K.C. is dying for his wakeup cup." She sounded like she'd known K.C. forever.

K.C. entered the kitchen, quickly grabbing one of the cups of coffee off the table. Both he and Derek dove into the box of donuts.

Jessie put out some cereal she had found. "You're a doll," she said to Derek with a smile. He looked up in surprise.

"Really? Why?" he beamed with pleasure.

K.C. appeared extremely interested in selecting another donut.

"Because you brought milk and bread," she answered. "We're going to have something better than donuts." She busied herself with the eggs, milk, and bread, and soon the smell of French toast wafted through the dining area.

"This is a side of Jessie that surprises me," laughed K.C. "I've never seen a woman who could eat so much and stay so thin."

Soon, French toast and a bottle of maple syrup were placed in front of them. K.C. and Derek piled up their plates with the unexpected treat.

"Jess, I've been thinking about how to change your looks," Derek said. "I don't want to do anything too drastic like dye your hair."

With a grin, he looked her over appreciatively. "And you sure couldn't be disguised as a man!"

She scowled at Derek. She was wearing some of the clothes K.C. had brought from her apartment. The warm spring day turned out to be perfect for her navy shorts with red and navy flowered halter-top and her red cardigan.

"I've got it!" she cried. "K.C. went to my apartment disguised as a street person. Could you make me look like one too? Most of the time people try to ignore street people when they see them."

"That's a great idea," K.C. echoed. "Jessie, you could be an undercover agent looking for drugs on the street. I could come along as your undercover partner."

"Some of the detectives know you, K.C. Maybe you shouldn't come."

"Don't worry, Derek. No one will recognize me when I'm done."

"Ok, let's get started." Derek reached for the case he'd brought. Unzipping the top he revealed wigs, theater paint, moustaches, beards, eye patches, false teeth and other cosmetics.

"I'll clear these dishes and make some space," Jessie offered.

K.C. helped himself to a moustache and went into his bedroom.

Jessie returned and sat at the table. "My first impression of you this morning wasn't far off."

"What was that?" Derek motioned for her to turn toward him.

"You looked like a peddler and just look at your treasures."

Derek laughed as he took hold of her chin and turned her face back and forth, eyeing her carefully.

"Hold still, Jess, I'm going to give you a few wrinkles." He began to work the makeup across her forehead and cheeks.

Turning and tilting her head as he worked, his fingers caressed her chin and cheek. His familiarity made Jessie very uncomfortable. He must have felt her tense, for an amused smile twitched at the corners of his lips.

He certainly is a dangerously attractive man. She was annoyed by the chills creeping up both her arms.

"Do I make you uncomfortable?" Derek asked as if reading her mind.

"Of course not!" she retorted trying to avoid looking him in the eyes.

"You're very attractive," he said evenly. "How serious are you and K.C.?"

"What makes you think there's anything between us?" She pulled her chin away from his fingers and gazed at the floor.

"Just something I feel when you're near each other. There's an electricity that sparks but doesn't quite connect."

"Oh," she was at a loss for words. She had felt that tension in the air as well. It was the "doesn't quite connect" part that was bothered her.

She had been attracted to several men since Jeff. She wasn't sure she was ready to get serious. *I don't want to be hurt again.*

"Well, if you ever need a shoulder to cry on, I'm available. Maybe we can make those sparks fly."

She didn't know whether to slap him or take him seriously.

Derek took her chin in his hand again, turning her face up toward his. All Jessie could see were his eyes looking deeply into hers.

"I didn't know putting on makeup was such an intimate procedure," K.C. commented coldly as he walked back in the room on Derek's last words.

Derek and Jessie turned as one toward K.C., their mouths open in astonishment. If they hadn't known his voice, they would have thought someone had broken into the apartment. He looked totally different. His hair now matched the moustache he had taken. The wig he had on was as dark as Derek's, only the hair was bushed out around his head. Even his eyes were black now. His clothing was even more disheveled than his previous homeless persona.

"Wow, what a difference!" she cried, pushing back from Derek. "I wouldn't have known you!"

"That's the idea," K.C.'s coldness melted. "Now, who is this old lady sitting in my living room?"

Derek tucked Jessie's pageboy hairdo under a very curly gray wig and turned her toward the mirror by the front door. She hardly recognized herself.

"Ok, now the finishing touches." K.C. laid an old wrinkled dress, tattered hat, and scuffed worn shoes on the couch in front of her.

"Is this one of those women's dresses I saw in your closet?" she asked him. "I thought maybe you had a girlfriend you hadn't mentioned."

"Oh, they come in handy for some of my jobs as well," he answered with a chuckle.

The shoes were too big for her so she stuffed the toes with K.C.'s socks. It only added to the authenticity of her part since she had to walk with a shuffle to keep them on her feet.

The dress may have fit K.C. but she had to belt it in, its bagginess helped the waif-like look.

"Are we going in two cars?" K.C. asked.

"The mole may recognize your car, we'd better go in mine. If anyone asks I'll say I picked you up to save parking spots."

"I'm getting a bit nervous now that we're ready to go," Jessie confessed.

"You'll be fine," Derek assured her as his hand at the small of her back guided her toward the door. "Weren't you ever in a school play?"

"A couple."

"Well, just pretend you're in a play. No one is going to recognize you. Besides, I'll be right next to you."

"So will I," K.C. interjected as he flung open the apartment door and took her arm, dragging her outside and down the front steps.

"Watch it!" Jessie yelped as she tripped over the baggy dress with her oversized shoes.

Four hands grabbed for her, surrounding her until she got her balance.

"So nice of you to help a little old lady," she cackled in a squeaky voice.

They drove off and the three of them were still laughing as their car pulled up to the police station.

Chapter 24

Detective Derek Alexander entered the Everett Police station, accompanied by a beggar and a little old lady. Since they were to be undercover agents from another town, Derek introduced them to the chief, the only other person on the force who knew what was really going on.

"Chief, I want you to meet Sally Jones and Mark Norris." Derek made sure everyone in the station heard his introduction. "Their undercover work brought them here. I'm going to consult on some issues they're dealing with."

"Welcome. Hope we can help."

Derek led them past the other officers toward his office near the back of the room. His office had a large window that gave them a good view of the men working at their desks. Once safely inside with the door closed, Derek turned to them.

"Ok, Jessie," Derek whispered, "it's up to you now."

The three of them walked around the office gesturing and pretending to talk. As she pushed past K.C. and Derek, she was able to look out the window into the room, taking in every person. There were people walking, sitting at desks, coming and going from other rooms. Suddenly Derek heard her gasp.

"The man who just came in the front door," she whispered. "He's wearing a police uniform and has…"

"Shhh, he's coming this way," Derek cautioned.

Derek beckoned K.C. and Jessie to sit. He picked up a pencil and started taking notes at his desk. Soon an officer knocked at the door.

"Come in, Jack," Derek called and motioned for him to enter.

"Sorry to disturb you, Derek."

"That's all right. This is Sally and Mark. They're on an undercover assignment I'm consulting on."

"Hi." Jack acknowledged them with a glance but quickly returned his attention to Detective Alexander. "Derek, this won't take a minute. I heard some of the men talking about a special detail that would be needed at a safe house."

"Really?"

"I thought maybe you'd know something about it."

"Why are you interested?"

"Well, I like that kind of work and wondered if you'd consider me for the job."

Was he talking about my safe house? Horrified, Jessie gasped.

Jack turned toward her, this time studying her more closely.

She sank deeper in the chair, willing him to look somewhere else.

As Jessie was shrinking, K.C. straightened to his full 6'2" trying hard to curb his anger. Here was the mole, standing right in front of them, pretending he wanted to help so he could get to Jessie. K.C. looked like he wanted to beat Jack into the ground.

"Thanks for the offer, but I've already made my choices."

Jack looked back at Derek. "Are you sure I can't fill in for someone? I really need the extra money."

Jessie saw K.C. begin to stand, his fists clenching and unclenching.

Derek rose quickly and escorted Jack to the office door.

"Right now I'm kind of busy," Derek concluded. Closing the door after Jack's departure he returned to his desk.

"I don't believe he was that close," Jessie gasped. "That was him!"

"I think you'd both better go now," Derek said. "We'll take it from here. I'll be in touch soon about the safe house."

They left Derek's office, keeping in character.

"I'll get right on that," Derek said to Jessie and K.C. as he walked them through the station.

Even in the midst of all the activity, Jessie could feel the eyes of several officers watching them leave – including Jack, who had stopped to visit with one of the other detectives.

"How are we getting home?" Jessie stood on the walk outside looking around. "Derek doesn't expect us to take his car, does he?"

"Didn't give me his keys."

"Maybe we could call a cab."

"One look at us and the cab driver won't stop."

Jessie looked at K.C. and started to laugh.

"You…laughing at…me? Take a look at yourself."

They laughed so hard they had to hold onto each other.

"We aren't far from my apartment," K.C. said when he could catch his breath. "I think we should walk."

"In these shoes?" Jessie held up one clunky foot and nearly toppled.

"I'll hold onto you." K.C. wrapped his arm around her waist and they shuffled off down the block.

Chapter 25

"Well, how does it feel being a street person." K.C. unlocked the apartment door and let Jessie go before him.

"Very sad. So many people crossed the street to evade us."

"How about the ones who just avoided looking at us as they passed," he offered.

"I've sometimes done that."

"Cheer up. An old woman like you shouldn't be so sad." K.C. teased.

"I can't wait to get this stuff off my face," Jessie sputtered. "I don't enjoy looking old." She was standing in front of K.C.'s living room mirror making faces.

"Yah," K.C. agreed." You don't look so hot as an old lady."

Jessie punched his shoulder. "That was rude."

"So is hitting a homeless man."

"I wish I knew what was happening back at the station," she muttered as she took off her hat, untied her clunky shoes and undid the belt that held in her oversized dress.

K.C. slipped into the bedroom and returned looking much more relaxed in chinos and a green polo shirt. His curly hair was still plastered tight against his head from the wig he had worn.

She turned to him laughing. "You look like a wire haired terrier." Jessie reached up and ran her fingers through his hair until the curls coiled lightly around his head.

"You could use some help, too," he chuckled. "You look like a little girl in her mommy's dress and makeup." He grabbed her hand and pulled her into the bathroom. Cold cream and tissues were sitting on the sink.

Gently, he dabbed the cream on her forehead and cheeks.

“I can do that,” she offered, reaching for the jar.

“I want to.” He gently pushed her hands away from her face. She stood quietly as he tenderly wiped the cold cream off with tissues. His hands caressed her face, seeking areas he may have missed. *He’s so gentle.* The feel of his hands sparked the electricity she’d felt earlier. The tingle that ran through her was growing in intensity.

The shrill ring of the phone startled them. They stepped apart. K.C. left to answer it.

“Hello? Derek? What did you say?” He paused as he listened. “How terrible. How did it happen?”

“What is it?” Jessie rushed to the living room.

“You think so? So soon?” K.C. held up his finger, signaling her to be quiet.

Jessie watched as K.C.’s eyes and brow went from shock and disbelief to a frown.

“No! I don’t think that’s a good idea.” K.C. was now angry. “She’s safe with me.”

I do feel safe here.

“Ok, I’ll tell her. We’ll be ready.” K.C. hung up the phone.

“Things didn’t go smoothly at the police station.” K.C. paced restlessly. “Go get dressed, and I’ll tell you when you’ve changed.”

Jessie was too afraid to argue. She ran into the bedroom and threw on jeans and a white embroidered gauze blouse. She could tell by K.C.’s voice that something had happened that wasn’t part of their plan.

He was waiting for her on the living room couch. She slid into his recliner and looked at him expectantly.

“Not long after we left, Derek told the chief who you had identified as the rogue cop. They decided it would be best to act quickly, so Derek asked Jack to come to the chief’s office.”

"So soon?" She was sure nothing would happen for a day or two.

"Derek confronted Jack about his involvement with Mrs. Spaulding."

"What did Jack say?"

"He denied it and stormed out of the office. Derek suspected Jack was trying to make a run for it and dashed after him."

"Wow, I'd liked to have been there to see the action."

"No, you wouldn't."

"Why?"

"The whole department was in an uproar over their shouts. In the confusion of the chase, one of the detectives, Sherman, pulled his gun, hoping to threaten Jack into stopping."

"Oh, no!"

"Somehow the gun went off, and Jack was killed."

"You can't be serious," she gasped. "Without Jack's information, what'll we do?"

"Derek is coming right over. You need to go to the safe house immediately."

"But why?" she jumped to her feet. "I didn't think I'd have to go so soon."

K.C. reached for her hand and pulled her back down next to him.

"It won't take long for Mrs. Spaulding to find out that her mole was exposed and killed. She'll know the police are on to her."

"Does Derek think she'll try to get away?"

"No. Derek is afraid she will do whatever's necessary to derail any more investigation of her." K.C. reached for her other hand and held them both in his warm grip. "That means getting rid of remaining witnesses. Derek thinks she is on the edge of panic. Right now, all her focus will be on eliminating you."

"I…I thought it was almost over." Tears filled Jessie's eyes. "I'm back in the middle of it again."

"The most important thing is your safety." K.C. pulled her to her feet. "Now go get packed."

Jessie turned away before K.C. could see her cry and hurried into the bedroom. She pulled out her purple duffel and started throwing her nightclothes into it. She hadn't had time to even unpack. *I hate this!* She swiped her arm across her eyes. *I want a normal life again. I need some time to sort out all the confusing feelings I'm experiencing.*

Jessie heard a sound from the bedroom door. K.C. had followed her and was leaning against the doorframe, watching her pack.

"Are you ok?" His face was a mixture of concern and compassion.

Jessie turned to K.C. "I just want it to be over. Do you think Derek would change his mind and let you stay there, too? Somehow, when you're around, I'm not as frightened."

K.C. smiled at her sympathetically. "I'll ask him, again, when he comes."

"I don't know what one does in a safe house. Can I borrow some of your books? At least I can read."

"Sure – as many as you want."

Jessie was slipping a couple of K.C.'s books into her duffel and zipping it up when the doorbell rang.

As soon as K.C. opened the door, he confronted Derek. "I have a question for you."

"No, you can't."

"You don't know what I'm going to ask!"

"Oh, yes I do. You want to stay with Jess at the safe house. I said 'no' once before, and I mean it."

"She'd feel safer with me there."

"K.C., Jess will be fine. I have four of my most trusted detectives working in shifts of two. There will always be two armed men there every day and night as long as Jessie is at the safe house."

What's wrong with them?

"What about food?"

"There is plenty of food for one in the refrigerator and freezer."

Don't they see I'm standing right here?

"She might get bored."

"She isn't going to be forced to stay inside. Where she's going, she can get out of the house. She won't go stir crazy."

Am I invisible!

"Will she be warm enough?"

"K.C., stop worrying. She won't be cold with this warm weather. Besides, there's a fireplace for the evenings."

"What if she needs something, and one of your men has to leave, will she be safe?"

"K.C., there will always be one on guard and my men are armed in case of trouble."

Jessie's life was out of her control again. These two macho men seemed to think she was just a pawn to move around in their game plan. Her anger with them grew until she could hold it no longer.

"Stop it!" she exploded. "This is my life. I want to know where I'm going, how long I'm going to have to stay there, and why K.C. can't be at least nearby as an extra safety measure."

"Sorry," Derek apologized, looking sheepishly at her. "We sort of left you out of this, didn't we?"

"Do you think?"

K.C. tried to put a comforting arm around her shoulders, but she twisted away.

"If K.C. goes, it will look too obvious," Derek told her, gesturing to Jessie to sit at the table. "Remember, he's supposed to be in Mrs. Spaulding's employ as well."

"K.C., were you expected to contact her?" Jessie asked.

"Yah. I said I'd give her a progress report in a week."

"I'm sure Mrs. Spaulding is somehow keeping tabs on his movements," Derek interjected. "She might even have him followed since she hasn't heard from him."

Turning to K.C., Jessie asked, "Did she give you a large down payment to find me?"

"Retainer. It's called a retainer." K.C. laughed and then sobered. "She did give me quite a lot of money. She's not likely to forget that."

"Things are coming to a head," Derek continued. "You're still safer with my men."

"But how long will I have to be there?" she asked.

"We have some paper work…get arrest warrants…file motions …things like that to bring her to trial. Don't forget, we've been following this enemy quite a while, so we've been ready to take the necessary steps. Maybe a couple of weeks, maybe more." Derek stood and went to get her duffel.

"You promise to let K.C. know where I am?" She met him at the door.

"I will. Once you're safely settled in, I'll tell him."

"Which of your detectives are you assigning to protect her?" K.C. asked as he joined them.

"My four most trusted," Derek replied, "Prescott, Pacini, Sherman and Rossi."

Derek turned to leave and Jessie suddenly realized that for the first time in four days, she would not be seeing K.C. across a restaurant table or in some compromising situation in a motel.

Had it really been only four days? The reality of the situation must have hit him too. She turned back to K.C. to say goodbye.

K.C. looked deeply into her eyes and gently lifted her chin with his finger. His head bent toward her and his lips gently brushed hers. Their first kiss was brief and sweet. Every part of her felt on fire as they stepped apart. The next moment, the door was closed, and Detective Derek Alexander was escorting her out of the building.

Chapter 26

Derek opened the back door of his car and tossed Jessie's duffel inside. Holding the passenger door for her, he motioned for her to enter.

Jessie hesitated for a moment and then looked up at the window of K.C.'s apartment. He was standing there watching. Derek followed her glance, waved, winked and gave K.C. the thumbs up sign. Jessie finally slid into her seat.

Derek closed his door and slipped the key into the ignition.

"I expected an official police car." Jessie brushed her hand across seat. "A bench seat, too. I didn't notice it before, I was laughing so hard, when we went to the station."

"She was a police car, a police Maverick, just doesn't look like it since I had her painted all black."

"She?"

"Jade – Black Jade – her color. She's one of nearly 400 units that had been packaged back in the 70's for the police. When the line didn't work out I was lucky enough to get this one."

"Nice. I can see why she's special."

Derek didn't seem anxious to go. Neither was she.

"I usually drive our regulation police car when we're making an arrest. Can you imagine what the neighbors would think if I'd come for you in that? We don't want a lot of attention."

"Oh." Jessie looked nervously around them. "Do you think someone's watching us?"

"Honestly I don't know. Worrying won't help." Derek started the engine. "This safe house isn't being used right now and no one, and I mean no one, is going to find you there!"

"It seems like this nightmare will never end." Her voice cracked as she struggled to maintain her composure.

Derek touched her shoulder in comfort. His gesture of compassion undid Jessie's restraint. Jessie was dimly aware that the car's engine had stopped as she collapsed into his arms in a torrent of tears.

Derek held her lightly as built up tension escaped through her sobs. Jessie's body trembled in the comforting arms that tightened around her and held her close. Finally her breath came in gasps and hiccups and her tears subsided.

As Jessie relaxed against his chest, she felt Derek fumble in his pocket. He soon produced a large clean white handkerchief, which he gently applied to her watery eyes and drippy nose. *Déjà vu,* she thought to herself. Pulling the handkerchief from his hand, she finished mopping her face, still sitting in the circle of his protective arms. He didn't seem ready to release her.

"I'm fine, Derek. Thanks for the use of your handkerchief. It's a bit of a mess," she said as she returned it to him. "I don't mean to be such a bother."

"You're no bother," he whispered. "I think you are very brave."

The look on Derek's face made Jessie nervous. His eyes had been focused on her lips as he leaned closer. *Is he going to kiss me?* Her heart quickened.

Abruptly she jerked away from his embrace.

"Derek, what's going on?" Jessie watched as he turned red with embarrassment.

"Jess, you are an extraordinary woman," Derek confessed. "When you were in my arms and so helpless, well…I found myself wishing…well…thinking… Never mind, Jess. I was way out of line. Please forgive me."

Jessie realized, that for all her defensiveness, these two men were getting under her skin. K.C. was physically powerful yet deeply tender. Derek, she sensed was passionate, yet mysterious and quiet. What had she gotten herself into? *Well, no harm done.* Jessie faced forward and glanced out the front window. There stood K.C., still in the apartment window, watching.

Chapter 27

Derek had made it plain that K.C. had to stay home and wait for his call. After three days of pacing, K.C. could wait no longer. Those days had been torture. He finished lunch and phoned the police station.

"Hello…may I speak to Detective Alexander?"

"I don't care if he said he wasn't to be disturbed. I need to talk to him!"

"What do you mean he's busy? Tell him it's K.C."

"Damn!" he slammed the receiver down. It had been the same yesterday.

K.C. was beginning to wonder about his friend. He'd seen Derek and Jessie in the car before they left. Why was Derek holding her? What was he doing? Did he kiss her? Did he take her to his apartment after all? He wouldn't put it past him. K.C.'s anger grew.

Where was she? He should be doing something to help her – not just waiting around his apartment, for Derek's call.

K.C. grabbed a book from the shelf and headed for the couch. There was the rustle of paper as he sat. Glancing down he saw something white sticking out from the cushions. He pulled out a letter addressed to Jessie Overton return address Tucson. *Must be from her dad.* Those four days and nights they had spent together seemed more like months. He felt like he knew her family. He thrust the letter into his pocket. Jessie had become a part of his life. Now, with her gone, it felt as if part of him was missing.

He knew he wouldn't be able to read. He had to find out why Derek was avoiding him. K.C. slammed the book shut, grabbed his keys, and nearly ran to his car. Entering the police station, K.C. was besieged with the chaos of ringing phones and people dashing about. He went straight to his friend's office where he saw him talking to two men. *Damn, he's busy.* Derek's back was turned away from K.C. as he waited outside the open door.

"OK, Sherman? Rossi? You'll take this next shift," Derek was telling them. "Your detail begins tonight. Relieve Prescott and Pacini around 7:00 p.m."

K.C realized these were two of the detectives that were guarding Jessie.

"Everything seems to be going well at the house," Derek continued, "so I don't think you'll have any trouble."

The men turned to leave, glancing at K.C. as they passed. One of the men was about as tall as he was and had thinning blond hair. His face was tanned and weather wrinkled. The second man was shorter by a couple of inches, solidly built, dark complexion. He wore a battered fedora. K.C. recognized the bulge of revolvers under their coats. At least they were armed in case of trouble.

K.C. stepped through the door.

"K.C.! Come in!" Derek invited. "I'm sorry I haven't gotten back to you. I've been swamped with preparations for the trial as well as seeing to Jess's comforts."

"It's Jessie's comforts I'm concerned about."

"You needn't worry. I've spent some time with her, and she is doing fine."

"You mean it's OK for you to see her, but not me?"

"Do I depict a tad of jealousy?" Derek replied with a grin as he waved him to a seat. "K.C., how serious are you about that girl?"

"Why are you interested?" he asked.

"Well, man, I've noticed your lack of commitment to relationships in the past. If you aren't serious about her, I might just find time for some fun of my own when things settle down."

K.C. saw red. Shooting out of his chair he slammed his fists down in the middle of the desk and shoved his face into Derek's.

"Watch your mouth, Derek." The words were out before he realized it. "I don't want to hear you talk about Jessie that way." K.C. noticed how quiet it had gotten outside the office. The other detectives were watching him. K.C. closed the door and continued more calmly. "She's not like those other women. I've never known anyone as sweet and vulnerable, yet strong and resourceful, as Jessie."

"Just as I thought," Derek said as he leaned back in his chair smirking knowingly. "K.C., listen to yourself. I think you have fallen my friend. It sounds like you love her."

In that instant, he knew Derek was right. The growing confusion of emotions he'd experienced while she was with him, the longing for her beyond physical attraction, the emptiness he was now feeling. Only one person could satisfy all the needs he'd been experiencing – Jessie! And he didn't know where she was!

"You did that on purpose, didn't you?" K.C. slumped heavily into his chair.

"Buddy, you'd take forever to see it yourself without a little help."

"What was that passionate scene I witnessed when you and Jessie were leaving my house?"

"Nothing you need to be concerned about, my friend. Believe me."

"Now I suppose you want to know where Jess is." Derek continued as he pushed a piece of paper across the desk to K.C. with the location of the safe house. It was the ranger station in

Billingsly State Forest. He'd enjoyed some hiking there last summer. It was only twenty miles outside of town.

"Can I go see her?"

"I still think you need to wait," answered Derek. "We have to have everything in place before we can arrest Mrs. Spaulding. We won't need Jess to testify against her until Mrs. Spaulding is in custody, and then it still may be a couple of days or weeks. If you are being watched it might draw danger to Jess by going there. By the way, have you heard anything from Mrs. Spaulding since she hired you to find Jessie?"

"No, now that you mention it. I wonder if she knows Jessie was with me. Her men haven't bothered me at my place."

"You might want to look into what's happening up at the mansion," Derek encouraged. "You have a good excuse to check in, and you might learn something that can help us here."

"I'll do that. And thanks for letting me know. She's ok, isn't she?"

"K.C., all Jess seems to do is worry about you. Man, let her know soon how you feel. You don't want to lose her."

Chapter 28

Jessie's mouth watered with anticipation as the enticing smell of popcorn drifted through the cabin. The microwave dinged, and she filled a couple of bowls for Detectives Prescott and Pacini and one for herself. They had been guarding her for three days now, and tonight Sherman and Rossi were coming to take over. This would be her last opportunity to share a snack and talk a bit.

She hadn't realized how much she would miss K.C. His solid presence was reassuring when Mrs. Spaulding's men threatened her. Jessie longed to see him. Her fingers tightened their clutch on the bowls in her hands. A wave of yearning overwhelmed her when she remembered the tenderness he'd shown when she needed comforting. *I sure hope Derek gave K.C. my location.* Something deep inside her knew that it was really important that he know where she was.

"Hi, guys, how about some popcorn?" Jessie strolled out to the porch where both men were lounging in rockers, gazing out to the only access road to the cabin.

"Hope this isn't too soon after lunch," she teased.

"You know us, Miss Overton, we can eat anytime and just about anything," Pacini answered.

"And boy, do I love popcorn!" Prescott exclaimed as he jumped up to take the bowls from her. "If you're going to catch any more sun, you'll have to do it soon," he continued. "It will be setting in a couple of hours."

The ranger station had been built thirty years ago. A rustic cabin provided living space for the rangers. For the present it wasn't being used which made it perfect for a safe house.

The 70ft. fire tower was a few feet from the cabin and loomed above them. A ranger could quickly go from cabin to tower for his daily checks of the surrounding forest. The tower's top was surrounded on all sides by glass, with seating inside for one. There was a circular map in the center of the room where the ranger could pinpoint the exact location of any smoke he saw in nearby forests. The tower room also had a phone that was kept connected all year round. Jessie had found all this out the day she arrived. She wasn't sure how long she'd be there, so she'd explored and learned everything she could about her temporary home.

The spring days were getting warmer so she took advantage of the beautiful weather by wearing her navy shorts again, this time with a short-sleeved yellow T-shirt. Jessie had gotten into the habit of taking a snack with her when she went up the tower. Sitting on the fourth platform, looking out over the treetops and thinking helped Jessie get above the troubles that had hounded her these nearly ten days. When the breeze was cool, she'd sit in the glassed-in tower. On warmer days she'd soak in the sun's rays on one of the five platforms that were connected by a zigzag series of steps leading to the top. This day the sun was fairly warm as the temperature reached the low 70's.

"I guess you're right, Detective, I'd better move fast."

Holding tight to her container of popcorn, she climbed past the first two levels of the tower and sat on the third enjoying the warmth of the sun. Setting her bowl down, she munched her way through the snack, and then she leaned back, closing her eyes. Soon she was asleep.

Jessie thought she heard a car somewhere in her dream. She woke to the smell of pepperoni wafting up to her. Pacini had driven to town and gotten pizza – again. She skipped down the steps with her empty bowl to find Prescott and Pacini wolfing down one of two pizzas. Jessie sauntered past them into the small kitchen and stood inspecting the contents of the refrigerator.

"Miss Overton," Prescott called, "Pacini got us a bit too much pizza. Want to help us eat it up?"

"I'll be right there." Grabbing a plate, she ran back to join them. Jessie had really enjoyed getting to know these two friendly detectives.

Later, as the detectives waited in their car for their replacements to come, she sat in one of the rockers on the porch. The sun was setting, golden rays spreading a warm glow across the tops of the trees that broke through their branches into shafts of orange light. The sun slowly sank out of sight. A deep longing not unlike hunger gnawed at her. She wanted to share the sweetness of this magical moment with someone special. A vision of Derek's black wavy hair and comforting embrace came to mind. But the moment blurred into oblivion as memories of K.C.'s square chin and tender caresses sent chills through her.

The last few days had been filled with such peace after the week of terror. She'd found real contentment in being able to separate herself from all that had happened. It also gave her an opportunity to sort out her feelings about the two men who had been thrust into her life.

With the sun's disappearance, the air chilled. Jessie reluctantly went inside and built a crackling fire in the living room's small stone fireplace. Drowsing by the fire, she began to relive the memories of the quiet time she and K.C. had shared under the apple tree by the stream. In the midst of fear and pursuit, they'd had a few quiet meals. Instead of fearing K.C., she now felt that she could depend on him.

Trust – was that what she was beginning to feel again? Trust K.C.? With what? His closeness ignited sparks in her that she found hard to control. Her body responded to that electricity. A burning desire for his presence engulfed her. If he could only be there with her, no strings attached, she would be content. She sat forward – wide-awake. The truth, like fire, crackled and burned its way into her awareness. Not only did she want to be with him, she knew she was willing to trust him with her heart.

Chapter 29

K.C. left Derek's office and drove directly to the Spaulding Mansion. At the gate he announced his arrival.

"Hi, this is K.C. Avalon. I need to see Mrs. Spaulding about a business matter."

A voice crackled over the intercom, then the gates released and parted. He jumped back into his Chevy and drove up to the house. Before he got out of the car, K.C. pocketed his .38. As he approached the front door, it opened.

A man dressed in black stood just inside.

"May I see Mrs. Spaulding?"

The man frowned, dark glasses hiding his eyes. He turned with a jerk and disappeared into a room off the hall.

K.C. stepped warily into the vaulted entryway and followed the man into a huge living room.

"Well, hello, Mr. Avalon," Olivia Spaulding greeted him from a wingback chair. "I was beginning to wonder if I'd ever see you again. Did you find my daughter? What about my necklace?"

Two men dressed in black lounged against patio doors on one wall. K.C. recognized his pursuers. He stood just inside the doorway checking out the exits. His eyes finally settled on the woman enthroned like a queen. There was no question as to who was in charge.

"Won't you have a seat, Mr. Avalon and tell me what's been happening this last week." She motioned toward a chair opposite here. "Since you don't have my daughter with you, I assume you failed in your assignment."

On her saying the word "failed", the men at the patio doors stood erect, hands moving to the insides of their jackets, alert and ready.

K.C. ignored Mrs. Spaulding's offered chair and chose one whose back was to the wall and within easy access of an exit. He scowled at the two men.

"I would have been successful if your friends here hadn't interfered. I'd almost caught up with her several times. However, I kept bumping into these goons and realized you didn't trust me and had me followed."

She looked pointedly at the men, both of whom became intensely interested in picking lint from their jackets.

K.C. continued. "Unfortunately your daughter realized it, too, and ran from all of us like a frightened rabbit."

"I'm so sorry, Mr. Avalon," Olivia oozed. "I just thought they might be able to help. I really wanted to make amends with my daughter and, of course, retrieve my necklace."

"At this point, I'm afraid I can't continue on this case. I lost track of your daughter in Oklahoma because of these…thugs." K.C. jabbed a finger in their direction. "You might want to hire someone from that area to continue the search. If you want me to return the remainder of the retainer, I will, but I had to use most of it for expenses."

K.C. watched out of the corner of his eye as the men by the windows drifted closer. He sat up straighter and smoothed down his jacket, feeling his gun secure where it could be reached. The crackle of the gate call box broke into the tension. Olivia nodded to one of the men to answer.

"Well, Mr. Avalon, I am disappointed that you were unable to help me. Don't worry about the rest of the retainer. Let's just consider this the conclusion of our business. I'll have to deal with my daughter in a different manner." She smiled as she rose to see him to the door.

A blue Ford pulled up as K.C. started down the front steps. A medium height man wearing a battered fedora climbed out of his car and met K.C. as he stepped onto the drive. Both men paused as a spark of recognition flickered between them.

"Mr. Sherman, please come right in." Mrs. Spaulding addressed the man entering her home. "I've been looking forward to seeing you since you called."

K.C. jerked the car door open, thrust himself into the seat, jamming his key into the ignition. He stepped on the gas and headed for the gate. His mind was churning and his heart beat wildly. He remembered where he'd seen the man, and he didn't like what it meant. His car was just reaching the opening when the gates cranked to a close. Apparently, Mr. Sherman remembered where he had seen K.C., as well.

I've got to get to Jessie! K.C. put his car in park, jumped out and started to push open the gates. Just as he was about to get back in his car, he looked over his shoulder towards the house.

The "goons" were almost on him. K.C. sprinted for cover in a grove of bushes and trees near the gate. A shoot-out here would probably not be to his advantage. He'd have to rely on his wits and his .38 only if necessary. Sneaking a quick look from behind a tree, he saw the two men split up, one going to the left around the premises and the other to the right, each with their guns drawn. *Divide and conquer was just what I had in mind. How nice of them to accommodate me.*

K.C. slipped from behind the tree and started to tail the one going to the left. Approaching twilight gave K.C. some cover, but also made it difficult to see his prey. Dodging from tree to bush, K.C. looked for a way to surprise the thug and relieve him of his gun. K.C.'s height didn't allow for many hiding places until he came to a massive row of rhododendron along a wall. Crouching behind them, he waited as the man came into view and stood six feet from him, legs apart, scanning the area.

The man turned and started past the screen of bushes where K.C. was hiding. When the man was three feet in front of him, K.C. lowered his head and lunged forward tackling him.

The two men fell with a crash, struggling together as K.C. tried to reach his opponent's gun. K.C. gripped the man's hand in a brutal hold, his other arm encircled his enemy's throat. A strangled curse hung in the air as the gun dropped at their feet. K.C. grunted in pain as his fist made a solid connection with the thug's chin, knocking him cold. After gagging him and tying him with his own belt, K.C. proceeded to hide the unconscious body behind the rhododendrons.

"One down, one to go."

K.C. could hardly see as he continued to duck and hide his way around the outskirts of the mansion wall. A chilly breeze whipped past him, and he shivered. K.C. heard a car engine start up. *Sherman must be leaving.* Derek's words were like a blinking neon sign in his memory: *"You start tonight. Relieve Prescott and Pacini around 7:00 p.m."*

The hairs on the back of K.C.'s neck prickled with chill and fear. He had to get to Jessie. The trees and foliage surrounding him created an intense darkness that made it impossible to see. Arms outstretched, he felt his way across the yard. He touched a rough surface. A tree. K.C.'s fingers moved over the surface. It was a large tree. He moved behind it. Suddenly he heard a "crack!" He froze. His adversary was nearer than he realized.

Another "crack!" Leaves rustled. Inching around the tree trunk he sensed the air moving and the soft panting of someone trying to calm his breathing. Suddenly, a figure darker than the night loomed before him. Without hesitation, K.C. struck out and felt his fist impact flesh. There was a startled "Oomph" and he struck again, this time higher. An arm swung past him, cracking cold metal against the side of K.C.'s head. Reeling from the blow, K.C. fruitlessly tried to grab his opponent's arm. *Stupid of me, I have to get his gun.* Finally he grabbed an elbow, shoving the man's hand above their heads, K.C. shook the thug's arm hoping it was his gun hand. K.C. slipped his grip closer and closer toward the man's wrist while he punched and blocked blows with his other hand and arm. As they struggled, the gun fired. Leaves and debris rained down on them. Finally, K.C. heard the gun strike the ground.

K.C.'s pleasure was short as a fist slammed into his jaw, and he fell to the cold earth. Before he could gather his wits, a foot swung into his stomach, doubling him with pain. The man's feet were near K.C.'s head. He felt the thug lift his leg for another kick, K.C. grabbed his enemy's foot in mid-air, flipping him to the ground. They battled wildly, exchanging blow for blow. Pain shot through K.C.'s head, his shoulder, his stomach. The cold ground was under him again as he fought back at the fists above him, hitting and slugging. The intensity of the assault overwhelmed him. They were fighting for their lives.

Visions of Jessie filled K.C.'s thoughts. He gasped her name, "Jessie!" He saw her brown eyes wide with fear. A new strength surged through him. K.C. rolled from under the man's assault and rose to his knees. In an instant he was back on his feet, fists flying.

Jessie's safety became his focus, reaching her in time his single goal. He fought like a man possessed. Hands, arms, feet all moved as he struggled with his assailant. The frenzy of action stopped when he found himself astride a very still body. Gasping for breath, K.C. reached for the man's neck to feel for a pulse. A rapid throb told him the man was unconscious, not dead. He wouldn't be coming around for a long, long time.

K.C. stumbled away from where they had fought, trying to keep himself from running into trees or bushes. Time was flying by and his panic began to grow. There was a pinpoint of light in the darkness. K.C. moved as fast as he could toward it. He could make out several lights like stars against the sky. It was the mansion. K.C. at last could see enough to get oriented and locate the front gate.

Suddenly a shout came from the woods. "Did you shoot him?"

Oh, no! The first man was loose. Abruptly, lights flared around him as the house spotlights were turned on. K.C., temporarily blinded, fell to his knees. Staggering up and moving as fast as his battered body allowed, he made his way around the trees and bushes until he saw his car. It still stood where he'd left it in front of the open gate. K.C. dropped to a crouch and slowly crept to the drivers' side. Cracking open the door, the dome light flashed on inside. His car keys reflected in the sudden light as they dangled from the ignition. K.C. slipped inside, quickly closed the door, shutting off the glaring beacon that announced his presence. K.C. started the engine, then gunned his way out of the gate and down the street.

Several blocks away, K.C. pulled off the main road and took a dark street that led to the outskirts of town and the ranger station. He madly drove with one hand, painfully pulling out his cell phone with his other battered hand. Blood dripped onto the steering wheel from a wound on his head. It took only seconds to call Derek's number but the phone seemed to ring endlessly until the voice mail clicked on.

"Derek…K.C. here. Get to the safe house quick. Sherman is one of Olivia's henchmen. Jessie's in danger, I'm heading there now. I pray one of us gets there in time."

Closing his cell phone with a crack, he pressed hard on the gas pedal. The landscape blurred as his car plunged down the road. K.C.'s only thought now was to get to Jessie. What if he was too late? His heart chilled with the thought and added to his determination. He floored the pedal and the car surged forward.

Chapter 30

Flames licked brightly around logs in the fireplace. A sudden crackling snapped Jessie out of her reverie. She savored, for one more moment, the deep love she'd discovered for K.C. His brief kiss goodbye, though tender and sweet, offered nothing beyond, a farewell. She shook herself and reached for *The Complete Works of Sir Arthur Conan Doyle* that she had started at K.C.'s apartment. She gently stroked the soft brown leather.

She'd become engrossed in one of the stories when the growl of an approaching car and the subsequent slamming of its door startled Jessie back to reality. She put the book down and glanced at the clock, 7:05 p.m. This must be the relief team. Jessie stepped out the front door where she could hear the men's voices coming closer to the house.

"Jessie," Detective Pacini called when he spied her on the porch. "We're leaving now, but I want to introduce our replacements."

Pacini turned to a tall blond haired man of indeterminate age, and next to him was a shorter man wearing a battered hat.

"This is Detective Rossi." Pacini pointed to the blond haired man who smiled engagingly at her.

"And this is Detective Sherman." He turned to the man in the hat. Doffing the hat, Detective Sherman made a slight bow addressing her, "Ma'am."

"You can sleep well with these men in charge," Prescott chimed in. "They'll be with you three days. If you're here longer, we'll see you when we relieve them."

"Thanks for all your care." Jessie shook hands with Prescott and Pacini. "I felt very safe with you two on the job." They entered their car, waved, and drove off into the night.

What a beautiful night it was. There wasn't a moon, but stars filled the sky with billions of pinpoints of white light against a deep black velvet background. She could barely see the fire tower in the darkness.

"Excuse me, Miss?" Sherman asked, approaching her.

"Yes?"

"Would it be ok if I guard you from the porch while Rossi catches some shut eye on the first watch?"

"That's fine with me, Detective Sherman. Do you want anything to eat from the kitchen before I lock up?" Jessie pointed inside. "I've been having fun experimenting with new dishes."

"I'd be obliged, Ma'am, for a glass of water. I'd also like to see where you might be so I can look out for you proper like." He stepped into the cabin, paused to look around the living room then followed her to the kitchen.

"Here's your glass of water. I'll just lock up behind you."

On the way through the living room he asked, "those three closed doors, where do they lead?"

"Just my bedroom, the bathroom, and a large closet," she offered without detail as she walked past him to the door and opened it.

"I'd like to see those rooms if you don't mind."

"Oh…"

"Is that a problem?"

"No. Since the other officers hadn't…"

"I just want to make sure you're safe in every way, Miss Overton."

"Of course."

Jessie took his empty glass and started for one of the doors.

"Hey…Sherman." Rossi stood at the bottom of the porch.

"What?"

"Before you take first watch, let's split up and check the perimeter before it gets any darker."

Sherman turned back toward Jessie.

"I'm safe in the cabin, Mr. Sherman. You don't have to worry."

Sherman joined Rossi as Jessie closed and locked the door. She had done so every night, but for some reason she was especially glad she had done so tonight. Something was making her feel uneasy.

She stirred up the coals in the fireplace, but its warmth and light were dying out. As cozy as it is, something's lacking by its not being shared. *I might as well get ready for bed and read there until I get sleepy.*

Pulling her nightgown from under the pillow, she made her way to the bathroom to change. Her hand caressed the brushed cotton fabric. Its tiny blue forget-me-nots and the kitten soft texture always comforted her. Jessie didn't know what she would have done if K.C. hadn't been able to get her more clothes from her apartment. The three quarter length sleeves and lace bodice helped keep the chill of the room at bay. The ruffled bottom edge swung around her ankles as she twirled about enjoying the flow of the gown. She hugged herself in wonder at this new feeling of happiness. Her love for K.C., though, would be cold comfort if she meant nothing to him. The thought stopped her in mid turn. She crawled into bed, propped herself with pillows, and buried herself in Sherlock Holmes. Suddenly she jerked upright. She had fallen asleep over her book, which now lay at her side.

"Time to get some shuteye," she said out loud to no one in particular as she snapped out the light and snuggled under the sheets and warm blankets. The soothing song of the evening peepers outside her window made her smile, and she drifted gently into a deep sleep.

Chapter 31

Sherman sat on the porch trying to keep his jittery feet still. He reached for his gun. *Not yet. Wait.* His fingers twitched in anticipation. All was quiet in the cabin and the car. He looked at his watch – midnight. Sherman slowly stood, took two steps and was off the porch. His feet crunched across the pebbly ground. He cringed, as each step seemed to shout he was coming. He lifted his heels and tried walking only on his toes. He stumbled and nearly fell. *Damn. Someone could get killed trying to tiptoe.*

At last he arrived at the car where Rossi slept. Sherman slowly squeezed the door handle, but, as the latch released, it made a resounding snap! Rossi sat bolt upright, instantly wide awake, the overhead light blinding him for an instant.

"What? What? Is it time for the next shift?" he asked as he turned toward Sherman who stood outlined in the door. A right fist to Rossi's jaw and he slept again, but much less comfortably.

After he pulled Rossi from the car, Sherman bound his hands and feet with rope they had brought. He gagged Rossi with his own handkerchief. Sherman opened the trunk of the car, then dragged Rossi's tall frame to its edge and managed to push him until he hung over the trunk rim. With a second shove the unconscious detective tumbled inside. Quietly Sherman closed the trunk lid and as silently as possible cautiously walked toward the house, flipping open his penknife as he went.

At the cabin porch, Sherman slipped off his shoes leaving them at the edge of the steps. He cursed the moonless night. His night blindness wasn't usually a problem, but he needed every bit of his eyesight tonight. Not a sound came from within the darkened building.

He'd heard Jessie lock the door earlier as he sat on the porch. *Nothing can keep me out.* He chuckled as he slid the edge of his knife between the door and the frame until it hit the lock. With a few skilled maneuvers the lock released and Sherman gently turned the door handle, pulling the door towards him. He tiptoed across the threshold. Much easier without shoes, he noticed. He turned and slowly closed the door behind him. He tried to remember what he had seen earlier in the evening.

The fire had died down and everything was pitch black. Sherman took a few steps forward. "Cr…e…a…k," the pressure of his feet on the old boards cut through the quiet. He pulled his gun from his shoulder holster. He had to be near one of those doors. Reaching out with his left hand, he slowly opened the door nearest the kitchen, peering inside. His eyes couldn't penetrate the darkness of the room.

He shuffled his right foot forward, then his left, his gun held ready, his left hand outstretched to feel his way. His foot touched something hard. Was it the end of the bed? His left hand felt fabric – the bedspread? He listened for Miss Overton's breathing or any movement at all. All was quiet. It was now or never. He took aim where he thought she was sleeping and pulled the trigger.

Chapter 32

Jessie was dreaming a wild and frantic dream where K.C., who looked like a frog, was chasing her. He kept yelling at her, "Wait for me! Wait for me!"

In an instant she was wide-awake and sitting up. She knew all the night sounds of the cabin, but the sharp crack or creak that echoed in her memory somehow didn't belong. All memory of her dream was gone in an instant as she strained to listen for more sounds – nothing.

Jessie slipped out of bed and ran lightly to the door in her bare feet. She stood, her ear to the door, listening while her eyes gradually adjusted to the dark. Her heart was racing. *What woke me? Why am I so afraid?* She heard a movement outside her door. Opening it a crack she saw through the gloom that the closet door next to her bedroom was open. There was the shadow of someone shuffling their way into it. *Who's sneaking around the cabin? What are they looking for?* Suddenly, she knew what this person was looking for – her!

Where were the officers? Where was her protection?

Jessie softly slid through the narrow opening of her bedroom door and raced on tiptoe across the living room, avoiding the creaky board she had come to know so well these last three days. Suddenly, there was the sound of shots from the closet. She bolted to the front door. Thrusting it forward, she was outside in seconds. It wasn't until her bare feet touched the frigid ground that she realized she wasn't dressed for the cold spring night.

It was too late to go back. Light poured from her bedroom window, then the kitchen and living room. She heard someone cursing and banging around inside as she ran to the detective's car looking for them. Staring inside she found it empty. The cursing voice was getting louder as the person made his way to the front door. It sounded like Detective Sherman, but how could that be? Where was Rossi?

"What happened, Detective Sherman?" She started back toward the cabin. "Did you see someone break into my cabin?"

"Yes, Miss Overton." The detective stepped onto the porch.

"Why aren't you wearing your shoes?"

Sherman leaned over and slipped on his loafers. "I didn't want to disturb you."

That's strange. All that light and noise. How could I not be disturbed?

"Where is Rossi?" Jessie stopped, but Sherman continued to slowly walk toward her.

"Conveniently indisposed."

"What?" Jessie realized then that Sherman's gun was pointed directly at her.

Without thinking she backed up, turned sharply and ran into the shadows of the surrounding woods. *Help! I need help!* Suddenly Jessie remembered the telephone in the fire tower. It was supposed to be a working phone. It was her only hope. She made another sharp turn and dashed for the fire tower. Goosebumps from the cold were prickling along her skin.

Her nightgown flapped about her legs. Picking up the edge of her gown she nearly jumped up the steps two at a time. Her feet damp with dew slipped on the first landing. Grabbing the metal framework, she was just able to keep herself from falling. Continuing to hold the handrail with one hand and her gown in the other she flew up to the second, then third, then fourth platforms. As she stopped for breath, she chanced a look back at the cabin. Detective Sherman was running from the edge of the woods back to the cabin frantically waving his gun. Jessie crouched low on the platform, moving back from the edge. She heard him calling to her in the stillness of the night.

"Now, Miss Overton, you can't hide."

His voice echoed lightly against the trees that surrounded them.

"I won't hurt you. I just want to take you back to Mrs. Spaulding. You left something at her house."

My purse!

"She just wants to give it back to you. Don't be a fool. You might as well give up and come with me."

What's the matter with him? Does he think I'd believe him after he shot up my closet, thinking it was my room? She knew who the fool was, and it wasn't her.

Where is Rossi? Sherman seemed to be reading her mind, too, as he yelled.

"There's no one to help you! Don't count on Rossi, I took care of him."

She hoped Rossi wasn't dead. Sherman wasn't an ordinary fool. He was a ruthless and dangerous one.

Jessie watched as Sherman continued searching the bushes and trees around the cabin. When he disappeared around back, she cautiously crawled up to the next level. Feeling safer, she stood and climbed to the observation level.

Sherman came back around to the front of the cabin. Jessie took one more step and tripped over the edge of her gown. Her body slammed against the wooden door, and the rattle of the glass windows in the tower room echoed across the treetops. She stood, painfully rubbing her shoulder. Jessie looked down and saw Sherman at the foot of the tower. He was peering up at her as she stood silhouetted against the starry night.

Jessie thrust the door open, avoiding the light switch by the door. As she closed it again, there was enough starlight for her to see the bench by the wall where she often sat. She shoved the bench in front of the door and turned to the telephone. Jessie grabbed the receiver off the wall and put it to her ear, a dial tone never sounded so good.

The hem of her nightgown was wet up to her knees and clung to her legs. Shivering with fear and cold she reached out to tap in 911. *Oh...no!* She'd never noticed before – a rotary dial! *They're in the dark ages here!* Her fingers moved along the holes and slipped into the 8. *Wrong dummy! The 9, the 9,* she kept repeating. The dial slowly returned to place and with an icy finger she reached for the 1.

Clang! Clang! Clang! The sound of running feet climbing the tower stairs filtered into her mind.

Hurry! Hurry! She nearly yelled at the dial as it slowly returned to its place again. Finally it was ringing. The reverberating footsteps drew nearer.

Click! A voice answered.

"Help!" her voice quavered, "I'm trapped in the fire tower. Tell Derek Alexander it's Jessie, Jessie Overton."

The dispatcher spoke soothingly to her.

"What is the problem?" the voice inquired.

"There's a man trying to kill me. I'm scared. I'm..." The phone dropped from her hand as the bench slid past her. The door behind her was open. The light switch flicked on, dazzling her for a second. Turning, Jessie found herself looking into the barrel of a gun. A panting Detective Sherman stood grinning wickedly.

Chapter 33

Sherman's gun hand shook. He gasped for breath, his idiotic grin never wavering from Jessie.

No! The scream echoed through her mind. *Not like this.* Jessie loved K.C. so much, now she'd never be able to tell him. Her hands trembled. Fear gripped her. *I can't die.* The thought flew through her mind. *How will I ever know if K.C. loves me?* It was at that instant her first moments of frozen shock slowly melted and her trembling grew less. *Get hold of yourself.* Jessie slowly eased herself around the map table until she was facing Sherman with the table between.

"This doesn't have to be so hard, Missy," Sherman cajoled as he motioned with his gun for her to step back to the front of the table. He took several steps toward her, opening the way to the door.

"Now come outside where we have more room. I don't want to make a mess in here." Sherman's grin had now become a leer. His gun dipped as his eyes flicked over her body.

Jessie caught her reflection in the glass behind him. Her hair was wind blown and her face flushed. She was breathing heavily from fear and the climb. With each breath the rounded mounds of her breasts pushed against the now partly unbuttoned nightgown. Her eyes widened with terror. *He wouldn't – would he?*

Jessie slowly took two side steps, leaned forward and dashed around the edge of the table. She was in mid-stride when Sherman grasped her arm, jerking her off balance. Pulling her back, she fell against him, then to the floor at his feet.

“You’re not going anywhere, Missy,” he chuckled reaching down to grab her once again.

“Don’t you touch me!” A surge of strength flowed through Jessie propelling her up. She lifted her knee hard between his legs.

Sherman doubled over in pain giving Jessie time to push through the door and scramble down the cold slick steps. She hesitated at the bottom of the first set of steps to look back. Sherman staggered out the door with his gun raised. He stumbled noisily down the stairs.

She’d reached the next landing when she heard the sound of tires on the dirt road as it raced down the drive to the cabin. She paused to look over the rail just as Sherman came up behind her. Jessie whipped around to see him raise his gun and fire.

“Click…Click!”

“Damn!” he grumbled as he threw the useless gun from the tower. “Wasted in that stupid closet.”

The gun fell to the ground with a crash, landing right at the feet of whoever was getting out of the car below.

“Help!” she screamed as Sherman grabbed her arms, pulling them behind her back. He started pushing her down the stairs in front of him as a screen.

“Shut up!” he spit at her. He pulled Jessie’s arms tighter. A scream of pain cut through the night.

“Jessie!” K.C.’s anguished voice came from below. She heard his feet pounding on the steps as he started to climb the tower.

Sherman also heard him, twisted her around to face him and reached for her throat.

“No more screaming!” he yelled in her face. His own face was wild, an ugly red. He was furious. His fingers tightened about her neck, preventing any more sound.

Help me, Lord. I don't want to die. Her fists flailed at the air striking Sherman's face, neck and shoulders. Her bare feet kicked at his legs. Lifting her by her throat, he pushed her against the tower railing. Jessie dangled from Sherman's hands. Higher and higher he raised her. She heard her nightgown rip as it rubbed against the cold metal handrail. Pain seared her skin. Her mind reeled. Bright spots shot through her vision, edged by darkness that would send her into oblivion. With all the strength she had left, she swung both her feet forward, aiming again for his groin. With a cry of pain, Sherman threw her to the side of the platform, clutching himself and cursing. Smiling weakly, she let the blackness of unconsciousness swallow her.

Chapter 34

K.C. heard a cry of pain as he stepped onto the second platform. He went to the edge of the railing, gripped the cold metal, leaned out and looked up, trying to locate the source of the cry. There was silence. K.C. turned and glanced down – a wave of dizziness threatened to overpower him.

"No!" He slammed his fists on the tower railing. "No…No!" He emphasized each word with a smack until his hands ached. *I can't let this happen again.* Looking up, he thought he saw a mound of fabric on the floor of the platform two levels above him. K.C. turned toward the next set of stairs. He resolutely took one step…then another. Dizziness overwhelmed him. He clutched both railings and forged ahead, going faster. The dizziness faded a little. He started taking the stairs two at a time. As his head felt clearer, strength flowed through him, he let go of the railings.

"Jessie, I'm coming," *Please be ok...*

The sound of feet running down the stairs above him made K.C.'s heart quicken. *She's ok.*

Midway up the next platform, he nearly collided with Sherman. K.C. barely had time to duck Sherman's kick to his face. With a thwack, the detective's foot slammed into K.C.'s left shoulder and his arm went numb. K.C. grabbed Sherman's leg with his right hand, pulling with all his might. Sherman fell heavily down the stairs on top of K.C. and they went crashing to the floor of the platform. Struggling to their feet, they faced each other.

"It's you!" spat Sherman. He swung at K.C., but missed. "I thought they took care of you at the mansion."

"You thought wrong, Sherman." K.C.'s left arm tingled with a thousand hot needles. He tried moving it. At least it wasn't broken. He used it to jab at his assailant while his right fist swung up connecting to Sherman's chin. The detective fell heavily to the platform floor. K.C. bent over and grabbed the front of his shirt, lifting him up before him.

"If you've hurt Jessie," he growled in Sherman's face, "I'll kill you!"

Sherman wrenched himself free. K.C. advanced on him, pounding his good hand into his left to get the feeling going again. He was ready to beat Sherman senseless. The detective slowly backed away. K.C. recognized the fear in Sherman's eyes. *He better believe me. If he's hurt her....* Sherman continued his slow retreat when suddenly his feet slipped on the dewy boards.

"Watch out!" K.C. reached towards the falling detective.

Sherman twisted around to catch himself, overshot the railing and fell screaming to the ground fifty feet below.

K.C. ran to the railing and stood looking down. Sherman was a dark unmoving form on the earth below. He suddenly stepped back, then cautiously leaned forward, gripped the railing and looked down again.

"I'm free!" K.C. laughed as he ran to the other side of the platform and looked at the ground below. "At last I'm free! Jessie!" He turned and sped up the stairs. *I have to tell Jessie.*

"Jessie! Where are you?" On the last platform below the lookout he found a body in the corner against the rail.

"Jessie?" Kneeling beside her, he gently lifted her head and shoulders into his arms.

Groaning, her head fell against his chest. K.C. swore as he saw rough reddish patches around her neck. *Why wasn't I here to protect her?* He thought his heart would break as he cradled her against him.

"I can't lose you, not now. " Tears of rage filled his eyes.

He brushed his lips across her forehead and rocked her in his arms.

Her eyes fluttered open. "K.…C.?" she whispered brokenly.

"Hush love, you'll be all right, I'll take care of you. No one will ever hurt you again." Carefully shifting his weight, he stood up, catching her legs with his left arm that was slowly regaining strength. Lifting her, he held her body against his chest as he turned toward the stairs.

Her arms rose weakly and she slipped them around his neck, her fingers brushing against his hair.

"Put…me…down." Her roughened voice made him cringe. "We're…too…high for you…to try carrying…me."

"My darling Jessie, it doesn't matter how high I go now. Something else is more important than any fear of heights."

"K.C.… put me down…I want to see your face."

Perplexed, he gently lowered her legs and steadied her with his arms. Jessie looked up at him. A cool wind blew around them as they stood high above the earth with its canopy of stars. He felt her trembling.

"Are you cold?"

K.C. was very aware of her thinly clothed body against his. His eyes moved from where the buttons of her gown had come undone to Jessie's damaged neck, then her pale face.

"No." Her eyes searched his. "You…climbed the tower to save…me?" she croaked.

"I was afraid I'd lost you."

"Did…did I hear you call me darling…love?"

K.C.'s eyes caressed every part of her face, her tousled blond hair, and her dark brown eyes so liquid and large in her sweet face. His finger gently, seductively touched her cheek following the outline of it to her lips that were slightly parted.

"I love you," he whispered softly. He looked hopefully into her eyes that were pooling with tears. Her eyes softened with such desire and love he could barely stand it.

"Oh, K.C.," she cried as the tears spilled down her cheeks, "I thought…I was going to die. I thought…I'd never see you again." Her voice grew stronger. "I was so afraid I'd never get the chance to tell you…I love you, too."

K.C.'s lips sought hers hungrily. He felt her respond with eagerness. His body tensed with desire. K.C.'s arms tightened around Jessie as he crushed her against him.

Chapter 35

Cruisers came to a screeching halt. Police spilled out, slamming doors, spreading out. Derek stepped from his car and surveyed the surreal scene before him. The cabin was fully lit with the door wide open. The only sound was a loud banging and cursing from the trunk of a car. An officer released the trunk; another policeman lifted a dazed Rossi out onto the ground.

"Are you ok?" Derek bent down to check on his officer.

"Hey, I'm all right, but wait until I get Sherman."

Derek stood and turned towards the body that lay grotesquely arranged at the foot of the fire tower. Another officer bending over Sherman stood and shook his head.

"I think you're too late."

Derek looked up at the tower until he found the silhouette of a person against the stars. Holding his breath, he walked quickly towards it, until he saw the one silhouette part into two. The two figures slowly made their way down the steps clinging to each other. At the last platform before the bottom, Derek saw Jess leaning heavily against K.C. She was wearing nothing but a dirty wet nightgown. Derek winched when he saw she was barefoot.

"Damn!" He dashed into the cabin and emerged with a blanket.

"Here…" He started to put the blanket around Jess as they stood before him.

"Thanks," K.C. said as he possessively took the blanket from Derek and turned to wrap Jessie in it. He slipped it around her shoulders, overlapping the edges in front. Swinging his startled bundle into his arms, he cradled her against him like a baby.

"Wait," Derek urged them. "The paramedics are on the way. Jess might need attention."

"Thanks, but I don't think I need them." Jessie snuggled against K.C.'s chest. "Can we go?"

"There are some procedures that need to be followed first." *I can't let them leave yet.* He felt torn.

"I'm taking care of her from now on." K.C. passed Derek and headed for his car. "I'll call you and let you know where you can find us when you need Jessie to testify."

"K.C., wait," Jessie protested. "I need some clothes."

"Oops, that would be a good idea."

They both watched Jessie limp quickly to the cabin. K.C. approached Derek, hands tucked deep into his pockets.

"I see you've been busy here," Derek looked expectantly at his friend. "Give me a quick report while we wait."

Derek listened attentively as K.C. told him what had happened at Mrs. Spaulding's and the fire tower.

"I'll write it up for you later," K.C. offered.

"So things are settled between you two?" Derek ventured.

"Yes..." K.C. was silent for a minute, then continued. "I was afraid I'd be too late."

"My friend – I'm glad you weren't. Just make her happy."

"I'm ready." Jessie had changed into a jersey, jeans, and windbreaker. Her purple duffle swung from her shoulder.

"I'll take that." K.C. reached for her burden and a piece of paper fell from his pocket.

"What's this?" She picked it up turning it over. "It's a letter for me from Tucson."

"I found it stuck in my couch. I was bringing it to you."

She ripped it open and read the letter inside. "My dad wants me to come see him. Can we go?" She looked at both of them.

Derek wasn't sure if she was asking his permission or K.C.'s.

"K.C., I need her deposition, then you can take her to her father's. Give me the address and phone number and I'll let you know when to come for the trial. I'll be the only one to know."

"Thanks, pal – for everything."

Derek watched as they walked hand in hand to K.C.'s car. When the car door opened, the dome light illuminated K.C. tucking Jessie securely in the front seat, then he leaned down and kissed her. Derek sighed as they drove off, disappearing into the darkness.

Epilogue

K.C., dressed only in his shorts, clutched the *Everett Sentinel*, looking once more at the picture and article that filled the front page. Police were escorting a woman in handcuffs out of a courthouse. Bold headlines splashed across the top of the picture:

Mob Boss, No Lady

By Carrie Evans
Staff Writer

A grand jury today convicted Olivia Spaulding of murder and an associated money-laundering racket. The local police have been keeping a dossier on the illegal activities being orchestrated through the Spaulding Organization.

Infiltration of the police department by Spaulding's organization prevented police from successfully bringing the powerful organized crime leader to trial.

Jessica Overton gave an eyewitness account of the murder of Edward "the Eyes" Hamilton which sealed Spaulding's fate. Overton is a Junior High history teacher at Inglweiss Academy.

Through Overton's courage and the protection of her bodyguard, K.C. Avalon of Avalon Investigative Services, an attempt on her life was thwarted.

Other members of the Spaulding Organization are under indictment for their parts in the murder of Hamilton, whose body was found buried on the grounds of the Spaulding estate. Evidence of other murder victims was also discovered.

Spaulding's sister in California has taken custody of Michael Spaulding, teenage son of the convicted woman.

K.C. laid the paper on the couch and strode to the king size bed, pulling back the covers.

"Hurry up in there, or I'll come in after you."

***

Jessie peeked around the edge of the bathroom door. "What did you say?" She stepped into the bedroom and looked shyly at K.C. The bruises on her throat were healed. K.C.'s watching over her at her dad's home was a blessing. Several months later the police were able to get everything in order. It was another week after that before she had to testify. Those weeks had been a wonderful time of sharing and growing deeper in their relationship. *Thank you Lord that Dad and K.C. got along so amazingly.* Jessie had never known such happiness.

They were now in another cabin, in another woods, by a rushing stream. A fire crackled in the fireplace. Jessie stood waiting…nervously gazing at the handsome man before her.

She watched as K.C.'s eyes moved hungrily over her. She'd taken extra care in preparing for bed tonight. She styled her blond hair into the smooth pageboy that he found endearing, the ends curling around her chin framing her smile. Jessie clasped her arms in front of her sheer but "not quite see through" yellow chiffon nightdress. Eyelet lace circled the neckline and dipped low enough to show the edge of her breasts. She was barefoot, her toes curling under in anxiety.

In two strides K.C. closed the distance between them. Lifting her clasped hands, he twirled her into his arms.

"Well, Mrs. Avalon, you look absolutely beautiful."

Standing on tiptoe, she gave her husband a quick kiss, but his lips captured hers in a surge of passion that held her there. An irresistible magnet of anticipation drew their bodies together. Any concern she'd felt had melted.

Jessie wrapped her arms around his neck. She had longed for someone to love her in every way. She had heard once that intimacy has to do with giving, not with taking. She knew now she had found the one person to whom she could willingly give herself. She wanted to show him how much she loved him, to immerse herself in giving to him, especially tonight, their first night of complete intimacy.

His arms tightened about her shoulders and pressed her against his bare chest. His hands ran gently down her back pressing her tightly against his stomach. She felt weak when their kiss ended. Jessie's arms slipped from his neck. K.C. lifted her gently, carrying her to the bed.

He leaned over her grinning. "No more running, Mrs. Avalon?"

"Not since I've run home to you." She reached up and ran her fingers through his hair.

K.C. turned off the light. The crackling fire with its dancing orange glow was the only witness.